IMPERVIOUS

IMPERVIOUS

A YOUNG ADULT NOVEL

A.J. HARTLEY

Charlotte, NC

FALSTAFF
BOOKS
WWW.FALSTAFFBOOKS.COM

To Riley Howell and Reed Parlier.

I will redeem all this on Percy's head," Trina Warren read aloud. *"And in the closing of some glorious day be bold to tell you that I am your son; When I will wear a garment all of blood and stain my favors in a bloody mask, which, wash'd away, shall scour my shame with it."*

The bell for the end of third period rang, and the class got to their feet so that Miss Perkins, their pedantic and unhelpful English teacher, had to raise her voice to one notch below shouting pitch.

"All of acts four and five for Friday, class," she almost screamed, "and yes, Mr. Shelston, there will be a quiz."

Trina rolled her eyes, but that was for her friends' benefit. She was good at English and was actually enjoying reading Shakespeare—even Miss Perkins's weirdo choice of *Henry IV Part One*—though that wasn't something she would admit, even to Jasmine. She got enough ribbing as a sci-fi geek and computer nerd without feeding the stereotype.

Jasmine groaned out loud, so Trina made a sympathetic face. Her friend was struggling in Human Geography and had withdrawn from AP World History after they did their project on medieval medicine and the Black Death. If she got lower than a B in English this semester, her parents would go up the wall. They were only nine months away from college application season, and Jasmine's mom and dad had told her flat out that if she didn't earn some kind of scholarship, they would oppose her going to college, period. They didn't have the resources to help her study art history, anthropology, or whatever at UNC Charlotte. Privately, Trina could sort of see their point, since Jasmine only wanted to go to college to get out of Treysville. But then Trina could see that point too.

Treysville was, her friends agreed, literally the Worst Place in the World: a rural backwater almost exactly an hour and a half drive from anywhere: Charlotte, Raleigh, even Greensboro. It was a town just far enough from the interstate to be convenient for nothing, a sprawling line of low-rent strip malls, car dealerships, fast food joints, gas stations, and diners. It was at one of those—Jimmy-Jack's—that Trina made a few bucks waitressing after school, with varying degrees of incompetence. It hadn't always been like this. Predating the strip, Treysville had a run-down town center with a church and a courthouse, and on the east side was a mostly disused set of railroad sidings that once served the now-defunct furniture business, but that was about it; there were a few farms, but mostly the school kids all came from the same nondescript houses, beyond which were equally nondescript trees and hills, scraggy and undramatic. Who could blame Trina and Jasmine for wanting out?

So school, which had been mostly boring, something that got in the way of Trina's reading, videogaming, and quiet longhand scribbling in the notebooks she hoped to turn into a fantasy novel, had become a trial by ordeal. Survive the ordeal and you were rewarded with escape into a new world, new possibilities. Trina tried to keep that in mind, but the trial itself seemed endless.

More of a marathon than a sprint, Trina's dad would say, an eye-roller if ever there was one.

Not for the first time, the thought of her father gave her pause. In the last few months, she had come to the pained conclusion that though she loved him unquestioningly, their positions had reversed since her mother died: he now needed her more than she needed him. It was a terrible thing to think, and left her feeling cold and hollow. Ungrateful. Perhaps going away to college wasn't such a great idea. And besides, for all her frustration with Treysville, Trina was, she knew, a little afraid of the wider world. She was a homebody. Just the other night she had caught herself thinking that she could write fantasy novels —her not-so-secret ambition—anywhere. She didn't need to travel halfway across the country to see what was in her head. She hadn't said this to Jasmine, who would laugh, or to her father, who might cry. She couldn't bear that. If she'd still been close to Candace, she might have told her, mentioning it lightly as if it didn't really matter, just to see what her old friend would say. Candace was grounded, sure of herself, not easily distracted. But Candace had new friends now...

"Hey, Warren! Nice juggling last night!"

Trina, who had been shoving her books into her bag, turned to see Kyle Martin grinning at her. Beside him were Steve Parks, another football player, and Colin Everett, a ratty hanger-on whose father was doing time for selling meth. Kyle mimed something spazzy, hands in the air and a goofy expression on his face. The others snorted like it was the funniest thing they'd ever seen.

"Ignore them," said Jasmine, putting a hand on Trina's arm.

"They take those plates out of your paycheck?" asked Steve Parks gleefully.

Trina looked down, her face hot and her hands clumsy as she tried to close the backpack.

"There's more to life than catching things," said Jasmine, a remark so surprising in its deftness and bravery that Trina looked up and blinked at her friend.

"Not for you there's not, Sears," Kyle shot back.

"Leave her alone," said Trina, her voice shaking.

"Ooh," said Steve Parks. "Check out the losers standing up for each other."

"Freaks," said Colin, making a simpering face.

"Gross," said Steve.

"We're not freaks," muttered Jasmine.

"You don't get to make that call," said Kyle. His face was harder now, affronted by their meager defiance. "Doesn't matter what you think you are. If we say you're freaks and losers, guess what? You're freaks and losers."

And then they were gone, laughing and high-fiving.

"Assholes," said Trina.

"Language!" said Miss Perkins.

They hadn't realized she was still there, and both girls stared at her blankly, amazed and outraged. The teacher stared them down, and they left the classroom at a brisk walk, jaws set till they were out of earshot, walking the hallway under the watchful stare of the school mascot, the East Trey High lion.

"She's the worst!" said Trina, horrified to find that her eyes brimmed with tears of anger and humiliation. "She stands there and listens to them say all...*that*, and then yells at us?"

"Total bitch," said Jasmine as they passed the gym and the steps down to the swimming pool, which had been closed for renovation since the start of term. "She's hated me since eighth grade. Says I don't apply myself."

"She's a bully," said Trina, hardly listening. "She's as bad as them. Losers. They think they are so smart because they can throw a ball around? Big deal."

They walked on in hot, loaded silence, all the way to the little room that was as close to a chapel as East Trey High got, though it was pointedly nondenominational and known as "the Quiet Room." Trina had never seen anyone use it except for storage. At the moment it was crammed with the remnants of someone's history project—a cluster of clumsily made knights fighting a dragon, though the knights were less *Game of Thrones* than they were *Monty Python*, and the dragon looked like Nessie.

"What happened?" asked Jasmine at last. "The *juggling* thing. What was he talking about?"

Trina deflated but wiped her eyes.

"I dropped some plates last night at Jimmy-Jack's. Three orders of chicken-fried steak. One of them had a smear of gravy on the edge, and it just slipped out of my hand. Probably would have been okay if I had just let that one go, but I tried to catch it and…"

"You lost all three?"

"I thought Jimmy was going to fire me on the spot."

"But he didn't?"

"He docked my wages though. So I worked all night for virtually nothing."

"Ouch."

"Yeah. Second time this month. Jimmy says that if it happens again, I'm out."

"Would that be so bad? It's not like you love it there."

"Need the money," Trina replied. "I just have to be more careful. I was reading a book in the bathroom and lost track of time. Jimmy said people were waiting for me to clear, so then I rushed. Lost focus. Hence the juggling. Just my luck those guys were in to see."

"You were reading a book?" said Jasmine, making a pained face.

"Arthurian legends," Trina admitted. "Knights of the round table and stuff. Totally cool and, you know, sort of educational."

"Probably not what Jimmy thinks he's paying you for though."

"I see that," Trina conceded.

Jasmine made a sympathetic face, then brightened up.

"You brought lunch from home?"

Trina patted the backpack she was half dragging along the polished hall floor.

"Dad's delight," she said, managing a grim smile. "Ever since I went veggie, lunch has become an adventure in cheese and dried apricots."

In fact, of course, she had "gone veggie" almost a year ago, but her dad hadn't been the one to look after her lunches then.

"Yum," said Jasmine, sympathetically. "Is it still gross outside?"

It had been raining since dawn.

"Yeah," said Trina. "It's a cafeteria day."

She said it resignedly, because that meant that the factions, teasing, and low-grade hostilities with the other kids would continue. When the weather was good, they could hole up under an elm tree on the corner of the playing fields in peace. Occasionally, Candace still joined them.

Trina had glimpsed her at the fair two nights ago. It was just a local traveling thing, some noisy rides smelling of oil, cotton candy machines, and a few of those try-your-luck games where the prizes aren't worth the price of the attempt. Trina's dad had taken her because he was determined to do as much of what he called "daddy-daughter stuff" as possible over the year and a half or so before she went away to college. He had been shooting cans with an air rifle when she had turned away, trying not to look bored, and seen Candace with Amanda Casey and Jill Armstrong. She had turned back quickly, anxious in case Candace's cheerleader friends saw her in her old jeans and a plaid shirt. With her dad.

Trina's dad hadn't really registered that Candace wasn't really Trina's friend anymore, and Trina had been terrified that he would spot her and insist they say hello, but Candace and her friends had been laughing at something so delightedly that they wouldn't have spotted Trina if she had been standing under a neon sign. So that was good. Trina and Jasmine made excuses, but in their hearts, they knew: they just weren't cool enough for Candace anymore, probably never had been. In middle school, that hadn't mattered, and the three of them had stuck together when they transferred to East Trey High, but in the course of their freshman year, Candace had blossomed in ways they hadn't. You couldn't really blame her. After all, if their positions were reversed...

No, thought Trina, defiantly. No. She would have stood by her friends, not traded them in for the cooler new model like old-fashioned clothes.

Jasmine made a left through a crowd of freshmen fumbling with their lockers, and led the way on past the gym toward the double doors of the assembly hall. The volume of talk and laughter seemed to go up with each step. Outside the hall some kids had set up an information table with bulletin boards advertising a school trip to Washington DC.

"Hold up," said Trina. "I wanna see this."

She paused to consider the planned itinerary and look over the brochures for the various sights and museums. She had never been particularly interested in politics, but the sight of the capital's imposing architecture fascinated her. She studied the glossy images of the National Mall, the pale stone of the Jefferson and Lincoln Memorials, and the Washington Monument itself, rising like a beacon over the city. It looked impressive, she thought, almost in spite of herself, a towering symbol radiating out across the nation like a lighthouse.

"You can go up the inside of that, you know," said Elliot Watts, a skinny junior who wore heavy glasses and, today, a bowtie with his short-sleeved shirt.

"I know," said Trina.

Elliot nodded. "Sign up if you are interested," he said.

"How much is it?" asked Jasmine.

"Depends how many people come," said Elliot. "Sign up and we'll email you some numbers as soon as we have a firm-ish head count."

"Are you flying?" asked Trina. She had moved on from the National Mall and was now scanning pictures from the Smithsonian's Natural History museum. One showed the skull of a rare two-horned narwhal.

"Train," said Elliot. "Takes a while but should be fun."

"Cool," said Trina absently. She wasn't sure her dad could afford the trip. Her mother's medical expenses had been ruinous, a nightmare from which they were awaking slowly and cautiously five months later. That they had to do so without her mother, all that expense eventually futile, only made the injustice of the thing sting harder.

"We're also selling stuff on the next table," said Elliot. "Fundraiser. The more we make, the cheaper the trip will be."

"Whatya got?" asked Jasmine, sidling down to a longer table staffed by Carrie Stevens and Latisha Price.

"School merch," said Elliot. "East Trey Lions sweatshirts and stuff, but also jewelry and stuff donated by local businesses."

"Wow," said Jasmine, impressed. She held up a carboard flap with a pair of dangly earrings on it. "These are pretty nice."

"Good price too," said Latisha. "They are mostly discontinued pieces, so you can't get them in regular stores."

"This is like a pawnshop," said Jasmine, uncritically. "How long you gonna be set up?"

"All week," said Elliot.

Jasmine raised her eyebrows in a way that said quite clearly that the trip was a possibility worth discussing. Elliot grinned, his job done. Or so he thought. Trina wondered if the deciding factor for Jasmine might have been Candace's carefully written name on the sign-up sheet.

"I'm going to bring some cash in tomorrow," said Jasmine. "These little dangly purple orb thingies are pretty cool. They're all glowy."

"Is that good?" asked Trina.

"Absolutely," said Latisha, grinning.

"Ooh," said Trina, returning her attention to the Smithsonian brochure she had been studying. "A sea dragon!"

"You are so weird," said Jasmine, affectionately taking her arm.

"What?" said Trina in mock outrage. "Nature is cool!"

"Very profound," said Jasmine, shaking her head, amused.

"I mean it! Look how cool that is."

"It's weird looking," said Jasmine, peering at the picture of the creature with its long snout and weed-like body. "And kind of scary."

"Only if you are, like, a microscopic shrimp guy or fish larva," said Trina. "Sea dragons are pretty small."

"How do you know this stuff?" asked Jasmine, steering her away and waving to Latisha with her fingers.

"Hobbies," said Trina. "Books. The internet."

They were passing the open doors of the assembly hall, which was empty save for a huddled ring of plastic chairs. Without anyone sitting in them, they looked oddly out of place in the huge room, like an ancient stone circle.

"What's going on in there?" said Trina suspiciously, stopping in the doorway. "Some kind of club meeting?"

She had requested the use of the hall for a week of *Harry Potter* movie screenings but had been turned down, the principal telling her that the hall was to be utilized for full school functions only.

"You going in there?"

A boy she didn't know was standing behind her, waiting pointedly. He was slight, preppily dressed in gold-rimmed glasses, and he looked annoyed.

"Nope," she replied.

"Then, do you mind?" He said it irritably, waiting for her to move.

"What are you doing in there," said Trina, peering at the circle of chairs, still half blocking the entrance, "restaging the Council of Elrond?"

Jasmine grinned at her.

"Oh great," said the boy, deadpan, "nerd comedy. I have a permit for the room, okay? Now, are you gonna get out of my way or what?"

"Wow," said Trina. "Rude."

"Just trying to get on with my day," the boy replied sourly.

"While ruining everyone else's," Trina said.

"Then go play Dungeons and Dragons or whatever it is you do to cheer yourselves up," he said, giving her a withering stare.

"Guess who just fumbled their charisma roll?" said Trina sweetly.

"You must have them rolling in the aisles in your mom's basement," said the boy.

His offhand reference to her mother, unintended and unknowing though it surely was, needled her.

"Asshat," she muttered.

"What? No more witty *Lord of the Rings* banter?" he snapped back. "Awesome. Now move."

He was shouldering his way through when Trina's phone started buzzing and the school bell started ringing again, though it couldn't possibly be fourth period yet, and there was a bang and a shout, and Jasmine was looking baffled and indignant, and the boy with the glasses was stumbling past her. He reached for the back of one of the chairs as if to steady himself, but it over turned. For a second it spun, its chrome legs in the air, and then…

And then.

H ow was school?" Trina's dad asked as soon as she got into the car.

"Fine," she replied. "The usual. Got into a fight with some kid in the hallway because I was *in his way*. Jackass."

"A *fight* fight?" asked her father, suddenly anxious.

She shook her head.

"A squabble," she clarified. "He was rude, so I was rude back. It was a whole big highschooly scene and was over in about ten seconds, possibly less."

"You had trouble with this kid before?"

"Never even *seen* him before. He just came in all *you're in my way*," she said, putting on a snobby voice, "and I was like, *excuse me?* and he was all *I have a permit…*"

"I think I get it," he said, pulling away from one of Main Street's three sets of traffic signals.

"Yeah, well. He just made me so mad. Got under my skin."

"Why?"

Trina shrugged. "Don't know," she said. "Made me feel stupid. Guilty, somehow."

"Guilty? For what?"

"I don't know. Getting in his way. Being alive. Who knows?" She shrugged again, emphatically this time. Since her father had become the sole parent, he tended to get over-anxious about her wellbeing. It was sweet but could also be exhausting. She followed up the shrug with a cheery grin. "Otherwise, yeah, school was fine," she concluded, hoping that would be the end of it.

"Lunch okay?" he asked with a half-smile.

Trina grinned. "Yeah," she said. There had been peanut butter and celery, a banana, and a raspberry yogurt. There was a wrapped thing of string cheese but no dried apricots. He was obviously making an effort. "Thanks."

"Good," he said, satisfied. "Got a lot of homework?"

"Not too much for a change. I said I'd do an extra shift at Jimmy-Jack's to make up for yesterday."

"Ah yes," said her father dryly. "The Incredible Plate Juggling Adventure. How 'bout we try and avoid a repeat performance?"

"On it," said Trina. "So, if you don't mind dropping me there now, I can be home by eight."

"You gonna eat there?"

"I'd rather eat with you if you don't mind waiting," she said, knowing it was what he wanted to hear.

Before returning his eyes to the road, he flashed her that old, familiar smile of his, the one that made her feel young and grateful. She didn't see it so much these days. When he thought she wasn't looking, he seemed to drift off into... what? Memories, probably. Things that had been good but now made him sad because they were lost and irretrievable. She got that.

"Package came for you," said her father, nodding to a parcel the size of her fist. It was wrapped in brown paper and jutting out of the open glove box.

Trina drew it out, frowning. Her name and address were

hand lettered in unfamiliar blue writing on the front. The package was roughly taped, and she had to pull hard at it to rip a seam along the edge. Inside was a black jewelry box and a single sheet of cream-colored notepaper with the same blue writing on it.

"Trina," it read. "This belongs to you. You will understand. A friend."

She cracked open the box and pushed the sprung lid back. Inside, sitting on black velvet was a necklace made of fine silver chain from which a tiny sword hung. In the center of the hilt was a miniscule blue stone.

"Cool," she said. "It looks like the Destiny Blade from *Phantasm Three*."

"From what?"

"A video game," she said absently, holding the pendant up and watching the way it flashed in the light.

"Who sent it?"

Her frown returned.

"Doesn't say," she said.

"Jasmine or Candace?"

Trina shook her head. It wasn't their writing, and Jasmine would have said. She feared she wasn't sufficiently on Candace's radar any more for gifts, but she didn't feel like explaining that to her dad.

"Secret admirer," said her father, grinning.

Trina flicked him on his arm and made a revolted noise, but her eyes were still on the necklace. She replaced it and closed the box.

"Not going to put it on?"

"Maybe after work," she said. "Jimmy doesn't get to see me try out jewelry."

Her dad grinned at her sideways.

"That's right," he said.

Trina took her backpack with her to the diner, the little jewelry box safely zipped into one of its many compartments. She was still puzzled by the anonymous gift and its equally enigmatic message. *"You will understand,"* it said, but she didn't. She wasn't sure that the sword charm was exactly the same as the one in the video game because the Destiny Blade was what you got at the end. You only used it to kill the Big Bad in the final combat sequence, and though she played the game all the time, she had only actually played through to the end once. Normally she just used the open-play function, doing side quests, collecting gear and pets. She had joined online adventurer parties from time to time, but *Phantasm Three* was largely her thing, a private retreat from work, school, and family. She didn't even share it with Jasmine, who was, at best, an occasional gamer. Most of the gamer guys at school were into sports and first-person shooters. All of that left her with no idea as to who might have sent her the necklace, which was just a tiny bit creepy. That was the real reason she hadn't put it on.

Still, it was a pretty thing, she thought, as she considered it again in Jimmy's kitchen before putting on her apron and name badge. She lifted it up to her face to study the detailing of the sword, and it turned as it hung, sparkling, mesmerizing...

"Don't be all day," said Jimmy, coming in from the dining room. For a big man he was surprisingly light on his feet and had a bad habit of showing up when you weren't expecting him. "If you're going to work, get on with it. And try not to bust anything."

Trina tightened her hand around the necklace so he couldn't see it, as if his gaze would tarnish it somehow. But as soon as he bustled off, muttering to himself, she looped the chain over her head, checked the clasp, and let it drop around her neck. She eyed her distorted reflection in the glossy tile around the sink, adjusting the little sword so that it hung blade-down between her throat and the soft cleft of her breasts. She wished she had a mirror. When she thought it looked right, she smiled, satisfied, and let go.

As soon as her fingers left the miniscule sword, something happened. The kitchen around her with its cooktop grills, ovens, and walk-in refrigerator seemed to sharpen, its white and steel surfaces brighter, its details more precise. It was like someone with poor vision putting on glasses for the first time, and for a moment, she wavered as if dizzy. But she wasn't dizzy. Quite the contrary. She felt like she had, in that very second, recovered her balance, found her stability, her focus.

She blinked, then pivoted slowly, conscious that her awareness of her surroundings was strangely heightened. There was a new precision to the way the familiar kitchen laid out around her, as if her brain—or her gut, because it felt less like analysis and more like instinct—was accessing the structural blueprints of the place, each finely marked with measurements of length and depth and height. She spread her arms and rotated, first slow, then fast. On any other day she would not have dared do such a thing, since she knew she was risking stumbling, blundering into a stack of crockery, or sending a tower of glassware scattering in a cascade of noise and crystalline shards...

Not today. Not in this one moment.

She felt secure, composed, precise. She stopped the movement with the same unlikely grace with which she had begun it, and stood, marveling at herself in the steel of the refrigerator door. In that instant she knew that it wasn't only her spatial awareness that seemed more acute than usual. Her nose was suddenly alive to the aromas of food and metal, detergent, and something slightly foul and rotten beneath it.

The garbage cans, she thought, turning to them. *And something else. Vinegar and ammonia...*

She inhaled, rotating on the spot, her eyes closing, till she faced the corner and tipped her head down.

Yes.

She opened her eyes again. There were two black balls no larger than pin heads against the baseboard by the door.

Mouse droppings.

She stared, caught between a range of conflicting emotions, joy and revulsion, surprise and its opposite, as if she had somehow always known this day would come.

The dull drone of conversation from the next room had sharpened too. She could hear Jimmy flirting with Mrs. Armsted, the sound of cutlery being set down on tabletops, and the creak of that one chair in the booth by the window. She heard someone laugh, and then footsteps. Jimmy was coming back.

He pushed the door open roughly and glared at her.

"I thought I told you to get a move on," he said. "If I'm out there taking orders, I can't be back here cooking, can I?"

"I'm ready now," said Trina, calm, collected. Unusually so. Jimmy hesitated.

"You..." He scowled and tried again. "You changed your hair or something? You look different."

It wasn't a compliment or a criticism, and he didn't seem to know what to make of the statement himself. He gave her a cautious appraising look that was almost suspicious.

"You need to get the exterminator in," she said, walking past him with such poise and determination that he shrunk out of her way. "Those traps you put out aren't working."

Trina strode toward the dining room, sliding her notepad and pencil out of her apron pocket as she did so, but his awkward movement as she went by had clipped a stack of plates fresh from the dishwasher. She heard them begin to slide, could almost feel the microscopic adjustment of their glazed surfaces as the tower shifted. She felt the movement on the counter from the tiled floor and up through her shoes, like electricity shooting through her synapses. She spun deftly on the spot, shot out her right hand, and steadied the stack before it could fall.

Jimmy looked at her stupidly, his mouth open, saying nothing.

2

Trina dropped no plates that night, and while she did pretty much the same as she always did, she was tipped heavily. She had more confidence, more presence, she thought, and her customers liked her all the better for it, smiling and joking, their eyes drawn to her. Even Jimmy complimented her grudgingly and with a watchfulness that was wary, almost fearful. She ended her shift jubilant, snatching off the apron and whipping it precisely onto its hook before stalking out as if she owned the place.

There was only one thing that gave her pause. As she had cleared each meal, she had found herself lingering over the trays of flatware, drawn to them, the knives in particular. She reached in and cautiously drew out a steak knife, feeling the shape of the handle in her palm, the way the fine cutting edge seemed to slice through the very molecules of the air. She could almost taste the tang of its metal in her mouth, knew exactly where the blade was keen and where it had dulled with use and rough handling. It was an odd sensation but was also strangely comfortable. More than that, it felt natural, as if the blade had become an extension of her arm, something that was bound to her on some impossible organic level. She held it out before her, and it was as if she had evolved or, stranger still, had grown into what she was meant to be, muscle, bone, and sinew indiscernibly becoming steel somewhere below the skin. She swept her hand back and forth, cutting the air, until she felt Jimmy watching her, and forced herself—with difficulty—to put the knife down.

At home she felt it again, the cutlery in the kitchen drawers and the knife block on the counter sang to her, begging her to hold them, to wield them. She barely heard her father's idle, end of day chat and excused herself from dinner early, so she could leave the knives alone, uneasy about how badly she wanted to hold them, to test their weight, their balance...

She almost ran upstairs, relieved to separate herself from all that steel, and closed the bedroom door behind her so roughly that the vibration shook a crystal bud vase from a shelf by her bed. She crossed the room in a single bound and leapt, adjusting precisely in midair, then absorbing the shock of her fall with one hand. With the other, she caught the vase an inch above the hardwood floor.

"Everything okay?" called her father from below.

"Yes," she replied, adding mostly to herself, "I think so."

———

She dreamed of a bird-headed monster, a terrible, reptilian thing with hard eyes and a long, sharp beak. It had monstrous, clawed hands and wielded a staff of power from which it shot lightning. It was coming for her, stalking her, blasting apart every obstacle behind which she tried to hide. She ran, blundering and falling, her old, clumsy self, while bells rang and her phone buzzed and the chrome chair she had unsettled spun on its axis as it fell.

Trina woke disoriented and exhausted, as if she had barely slept at all.

"You okay?" her father asked, over bagels and garden veggie cream cheese. "Maybe you should take the day off school."

"Nope," she said, needing to douse his concern as quickly as possible. "I'm fine. And I've got a test in bio."

"Shot of coffee? Wake you up a bit?"

Trina made a face. She hated coffee, as he well knew.

"I'll get a Coke or something at school," she said. "Just need something to help me focus."

She avoided looking at the kitchen drawer where the knives were calling to her.

Jasmine spotted her outside the bathrooms by Reception.

"So," she said, "Marvel movie marathon tonight, or *Buffy* season five?"

"I don't know," said Trina. "I'm pretty beat. Let's see how I am doing by the end of the day. If I'm awake enough to get my homework done early… What?"

"You look… I don't know. Different?"

"Like I said, lousy night's sleep," said Trina, grinning. "But thanks for drawing attention to my state of near-death. I'd appreciate it if you could go a little easy on the astonishment that I'm walking around."

"No!" said Jasmine. "I didn't mean different, *bad*. It's a good different. You seem, I don't know, taller, more assured."

"Pretty sure I didn't grow overnight," said Trina, though she looked away as she spoke. She was wearing the sword necklace under her shirt.

"So, what gives?"

"Well, I have a secret admirer, or so my dad thinks, and I didn't smash anything at Jimmy-Jack's last night, so maybe I'm just feeling more competent than usual."

"Secret admirer?" Jasmine exclaimed. "Spill!"

Trina hesitated, but her friend's open, beaming face was impossible to deny. She wondered if she would be as generous, as utterly lacking in envy if their positions were reversed. She fished inside her shirt and plucked the necklace out, explaining about the anonymous box and its cryptic note. Jasmine leaned into study the necklace, eyes tight, mouth opened in a caricature of curiosity. She smelled of soap, and her shampoo had a whiff of strawberry to it.

"Woah," she said. "Who do you think it's from?"

"Got me," said Trina, shrugging and leading the way down the bustling corridor to their first class. They had been careful to pick the same classes this semester after barely seeing each other the previous year. "Weird, huh? I mean, I really have absolutely no idea. I kinda thought that when you got a gift from a secret admirer, you usually had a pretty good idea who sent it."

"I have no experience in these matters," said Jasmine with mock seriousness. "I will now speculate wildly."

"Please don't."

"Could be Tyler Mack who sits behind us in bio. He's totally into you."

"He's totally not, and I don't have him down as a *Phantasm Three* player or, for that matter, a cryptic note writer. If it was from him, he'd have announced it in eight-foot neon letters carried by a marching band."

"Who then?"

"See above, re: me not having a clue."

Jasmine pouted but found a silver lining, as she tended to.

"I'm going to scrutinize every guy who looks at you today," she said. "You just go about your business being all ho-hum normal, and I will be your James Bond eyes, only without the cocktails and tux."

"What makes you think it's a guy?" said Trina archly.

"Good point!" said Jasmine. "A mystery girl. Interesting."

"You are enjoying this way too much," said Trina, though she smiled as she said it, because Jasmine's response made the whole thing feel fun and playful and not weird and life altering.

The hallways were busier than usual, and the sheer volume of people made Trina gasp. It wasn't that there were more people around today: she just felt more aware of them than usual, the sounds of their feet and voices, the smells of their bodies, deodorants, and perfumes. They crowded her like pressure waves.

"You doing all right?" said Jasmine. "You look a bit…"

"Yeah, just…need a minute."

Trina frowned, eyes closing, finger and thumb pressed to the bridge of her nose as if forcing something into her forehead. When she felt more composed, more focused, she opened her eyes again and found Jasmine watching, her face a mask of concern.

"What's going on?" she asked.

"Just tired," Trina said. "I should pop a couple of Advil."

She was about to start walking again when she spotted someone who seemed to consider her as he passed: the boy in the gold-rimmed glasses she had bickered with the day before. He stared at her unsmiling as he passed.

"Who is that?" she asked, turning to watch him go.

"Don't know his name," said Jasmine. "He's new. Trans-ferred from Charlotte."

"Moved here from Charlotte?" Trina said, aghast.

"I know, right? No wonder he's so miserable."

But he hadn't looked miserable exactly, Trina thought. Yesterday he had looked sour and condescending and hostile. Today he merely looked...empty. His skin was waxy, and his eyes were dead. Like there was no one inside. As they made their way to class, Trina told herself she was imagining things, but her mind kept coming back to the strange boy's blank, appraising stare, and though the room was warm, she shuddered as if caught in a chilly draught.

She felt again that unreasonable sense of wrongness, of guilt. She scowled, annoyed with herself but determined not to say anything to Jasmine because her friend would say what she always said, that Trina worried too much about what people thought of her, that she was too bent on avoiding conflict. It was all true. Her spat with the boy yesterday had been one of those rare moments where she had argued mostly out of surprise that someone could be so unpleasant with so little cause. She'd called him an asshat spontaneously, because he had shocked it out of her. If she had had time to think, she would have said nothing, and on most days would have had to repress the urge to go after him and apologize.

Not today though. She felt different today, more settled in herself. The momentary sense of guilt was, she decided, nonsense, a stupid remnant of her former self. She pushed it away.

It turned out that the boy with the dead eyes wasn't the only new kid at East Trey High. Trina met the other in the library after lunch while she was working on her English assignment: she hadn't given up on the Marvel/*Buffy* marathon at Jasmine's house.

"Miles to go before I sleep," she muttered as she found her page.

She didn't know he was there at first. Her face was thrust into a book so deeply that it took a while to notice that the shadow that had slid onto the page was not moving. She looked up to find the new boy looming over her. The structure of his face was so sharp that the afternoon light cast deep, hollowing shadows around his eyes and jaw. It made him look striking in a broody sort of way, but also almost sickly. His hair was black and shaggy, while his eyes were large and a green so dark they almost matched his hair. He was leaning silently on the other side of the desk, his eyes fixed on her.

Trina's senses screamed, a cacophony of confused impulses, but the one that cried out loudest was alarm. She pursed her lips and forced herself to hold his gaze.

"Can I help you?" she said.

"I think it's rather the other way around," said the boy. His voice was odd. Not local. Possibly not even American.

Trina snorted. "That may be the worst pick up line I have ever heard," she said, genuinely amused in spite of the chaos of feelings.

"It's not a line," he said.

"Sure sounded like one."

The boy took his eyes off her at last, flashed them around the library, and sighed. "Can we start again?" he said.

"Start what?" said Trina, not giving an inch.

The boy stepped back, hands half raised in surrender. "Fine," he said. "But tell me one thing."

"What's that?" said Trina, her face like slate.

"Are you wearing it?"

Her confusion lasted less than a second, then her hand went instinctively to her throat.

"Don't take it off!" said the boy, suddenly urgent.

"If you think I'm wearing it for you, you've got another thing coming," she said, reaching round to unclasp it. "I don't even know you."

"I said don't take it off," he whispered, leaning forward and actually seizing her hand.

Trina shook him off and got to her feet. "Who do you think you are?" she demanded. "You don't know me. I sure as hell don't know you."

"That's true," he said, calmer now.

The response took the edge off her fury.

"Well then," she said.

"We don't know each other," he repeated.

"But you sent me...?" She snatched her hand from the chain, suddenly unwilling even to show it to him.

"Yes," he said. "It belongs to you."

The words from the note stopped her, but she rediscovered her outrage.

"It doesn't," she said, and now she did take it off and thrust it toward him. "I've never seen it before."

"I know," he said, keeping his hands away from hers. "But it is yours nonetheless."

"You're talking nonsense," said Trina.

"Yeah?" said the boy, leaning in close again. "Have you ever worn anything that fit you more perfectly?"

"What?" she gasped. "It's a necklace. Pretty much one size fits all, I'd say."

"You know what I mean."

And the truth was, she did. Taking it off had been a wild gesture, but it had pained her all the same, as if she had torn away a strip of skin. Worse, whatever metaphorical wound had been opened when she took the chain from round her neck, the aftermath was worse. Somehow, inexplicably, the world had dulled a little. Its colors had paled, its scents had evaporated, her hearing had numbed like she was on a plane or battling flu. She felt muffled and, what was worse, she immediately knew that this was how she had always felt.

Till she had started wearing the necklace.

This was normal. This was ordinary. The necklace made her...special. She had known it before but had ignored it because the truth of the thing made no sense and her brain wouldn't let it in.

"Put it back on," said the boy. "It's important."

She stared at him, wanting to do what he said, but refusing to give in.

"It won't hurt you," he said, gentle now. "Quite the contrary. And you may as well: no one else can wear it."

She considered that doubtfully, then, on impulse, laced it around her neck once more. Immediately the heightened world returned, so that she gasped with the surge of sensation as the library came into sharper focus again.

"Who are you?" she said.

"I'm Percy," he said, extending his hand.

"Like Hotspur," Trina replied, not thinking.

"What?"

"Character in a play we're reading in English," said Trina, waving the remark away and wishing she hadn't made it. "I'm Trina."

"Yeah, I know," he said.

"Right."

"I'm new."

"No kidding," she replied, considering his hand for a long moment before taking it and giving it a peremptory shake. "Did you transfer from Charlotte too? You must really hate your parents..."

But he was shaking his head and smiling wide enough to show even white teeth.

"No," he said. "Transferred from Raleigh. Deliberately. I came to see you."

Trina blinked and leaned back a little.

"Okay," she said, frowning. "Again with the lines..."

"No," he said again. "I mean it. I came to see you and give you that." He nodded at the necklace. "But I also have to explain how to use it, and we don't have a lot of time."

His earnestness unnerved her, and she pulled away, actually leaning back, those few extra inches as good as a wall.

"Yeah, I don't know what you want," she said, "and I'm grateful for the necklace, which is real pretty, but I don't owe you anything for it. If you think I do, you can take it back. Maybe I'll see you around."

And she turned away.

"I've seen your dreams," he said, his voice a notch harder, shriller.

She stopped, mostly from anger at his effrontery, his presumption, but she revolved to face him all the same.

"Like I said," she said, her voice low and dangerous, "you don't know me. You sure as hell don't know what goes on in my head when I'm asleep."

"I know about the beaked monster," he replied coolly. "I know about the staff of power he wields. I know that they are real, and they are coming."

Trina opened her mouth, but words failed her.

"You want to know how I know?" said the boy. He yanked his t-shirt up as high as his chest. The flesh below it was seared and blistered from his belt buckle to his sternum, the skin blackened and flaking on the outside, red and raw in the center. At the heart of what looked horribly like a massive burn was a terrible hole, several inches across, dark, poisonous, and glistening inside.

Trina stared in horror, realizing that she had been able to smell the rawness of the injury before. No wonder he looked unwell.

"Oh my God," she gasped. "You need to be in a hospital."

"They can't do anything about it," he said, dropping the hem of his shirt again to hide the horror beneath.

"Of course they can!" Trina retorted. "We should go. I'll call an ambulance…"

"No!" he said again, and though he reached for her with one strong hand, it was his eyes that stopped her, for they were full of pain and a deep, potent conviction. "This is a wound made by the staff of power. It is a magical injury, and no human hospital can fix it."

Trina stared at him.

"You're insane," she said, though her voice lacked all conviction. She said it because it had to be said, because the reality she had known all her life demanded it, but she knew, as soon as the words were out, that she was wrong. The rules of the reality she had known no longer applied.

It was as if he had read her thoughts, because Percy, if that was indeed his name, did not bother to contradict her. He stared long and hard at her, and then he sank into the chair again as if exhausted beyond measure.

"I cannot fight the thing that is coming," he said. "You may be able to. I do not know if you can defeat it, but I will help where I can."

"Wait. What? I'm not fighting anything! I'm going to take my bio test and do my paper on *Henry the Fourth*, and I'm going to prepare my college applications and maybe, *maybe*, if I'm really lucky, I might get into Chapel Hill and then…"

But Percy was shaking his head.

"First, you fight," he said. "If you survive…"

"If I *survive*?"

"Yes, if you survive, then you can deal with the other stuff."

"This is crazy. You've got the wrong person. I'm not fighting for anything."

"You must."

"Oh yeah? And why's that?"

He smiled then, a sad, distant smile that sucked all the air out of the room.

"Because if you don't," he said, "then everybody dies."

3

Trina's biology test went badly. She wouldn't get her score for a few days, but she knew her head hadn't been in it, and she had blanked on material she'd known inside out when she'd done the mock test a couple of days ago. It was Percy, she told herself through gritted teeth. All his crazy talk about swords and monsters. He had gotten into her head, and she couldn't think straight. She was so frustrated with herself as she left the classroom that she considered yanking the necklace from her head and tossing it in the trash.

But she didn't.

However lunatic it all sounded, however strange and daunting his tales of destiny and battles to come, she felt a sense of purpose and being that she never had before. Since she had first put on the necklace, she had felt more herself than at any other time in her life, and while that was clearly a nonsense statement, it made sense to her. The Trina she had been was a Trina in waiting, a student or apprentice: lacing the sword necklace around her throat had felt like graduation or, to use another, more promising term, like commencement. Whatever her new life would bring, she had set out upon the path, and she couldn't turn back now.

None of this made her any less mad at Percy for disturbing her reality or throwing her sense of what she knew and who she was into question, and she avoided him all day. Jasmine had band after school, and Candace, in so far as it mattered, had cheerleading, so as soon as the final bell rang, Trina slid out and headed for home.

As she walked along Main Street, her hand strayed to the chain around her neck, and her fingertips explored the molding of the miniature sword. It was just a necklace with a charm on it, a few grams of nicely worked metal: nothing more. It was true that her senses still felt curiously heightened, but there had to be a more rational explanation for that. She thought back over the last few days, trying to spot some shift in her diet or health that might account for the way the world seemed to explain itself to her. Maybe it was a tumor in her head, something that had squeezed some disused part of her brain into action before becoming lethal...

She felt a pull in her peripheral vision and saw a window display of hunting knives. The stark red signs shouted, "Gold. Guns. Tools. Jewelry. Lay-Away. Instant Cash."

A pawnshop. She had never been in one. She stopped, considering the knives in the display case, wanting to test their handles in her hand, see the sun flash on their blades. She looked deliberately away, and her eyes found the sign over the shop door.

Jewelry.

She pushed the door open, and a bell jangled. Though she had barely noticed from outside, the windows were tinted with a green film designed to stop the goods from being bleached by sunlight. It gave the interior of the shop a curiously submarine feel, the light a shifting dull emerald color.

It was like stepping into a fish tank. The store was haphazardly laid out, as if its shape was constantly evolving as new product came in. The aisles between displays were cramped. On her right was a wall of hammers, wrench sets, and power tools, on her left, shelves of pots and pans. Two men behind the counter, one white, one black, both tattooed, paused mid-conversation and considered her.

"Help you find something, little lady?" said the white man. He was thin and sinewy, wearing a sleeveless shirt that showed long, veiny arms. He was bald but sported a pale gold handlebar moustache, stained nicotine yellow around the mouth. He smiled at her, but there had been the merest flash of amusement between the two men as she came in, and Trina was immediately on her guard.

"I just wondered if you could look at something for me," she said. "Tell me what it's worth."

"Surely," he replied. "Whatya got?"

She sensed the other man's eyes fixed on her, but she stepped up to the counter and, with a surge of resolution, swept the necklace off and laid it on the glass, beneath which were boxes of coins, medals, and rings all with hand-lettered tags and prices.

Immediately the world dulled, so much so that she wanted to snatch the necklace back, but she steeled herself and spoke. "I don't want to sell it, but I thought I'd see what it was worth," she said. "Just in case."

"Alrighty then," said the white man, fishing in a drawer and pulling out a bulbous lens that he screwed into his right eye socket. He pulled the necklace toward him, turned on a desk lamp, which cut through the greenish glow of the shop, and leaned over it.

"Silver," he said, examining the chain. "Decent. Nothing special. Give you twenty bucks for that. The pendant..." His voice trailed off, and he licked his lips. Without looking up, he said, "Jerry, come see this."

The black man, who was also bald but heavier, slid over on a wheeled stool, and they traded off the jeweler's loupe. As the second man leaned in to study the necklace, the white man looked first at Trina, and then at his partner. His face was carefully blank, but Trina thought he was…interested.

"What you make of that?" he said.

"The stone," said Jerry.

"Exactly my point," said the other man.

"It's small, but it's like there's a light inside it. Not just reflection. Too small for an LED, and there's no power source."

"You ever seen anything like that before?"

"Not rightly sure. Don't reckon."

"Where'd you get this, miss?" said the white man. He was standing up very slowly and carefully.

Trina felt a rising tide of watchfulness and anxiety.

"I could make you a nice deal for that," said the guy with the moustache, his eyes boring into hers.

"That's okay," said Trina. "I was just…"

"Easy there, little lady," he answered. His buddy was still gazing through the lens as if entranced. "I reckon we can come to a deal that will satisfy all parties."

Trina held his eyes, deliberately not looking at the necklace, then made a long, sweeping grab for it. The man with the loupe was engrossed in his examination and didn't respond till she had the chain in her fist, but the white man was already sliding over the counter.

There was something serpentine about the movement. Trina took a long step back and ducked her head through the loop of the necklace. The world sharpened and clarified, but so did the pawnbrokers. The one with the moustache who was sliding toward her over the counter was now impossibly liquid, boneless. He poured over the glass cabinet, pooled briefly on the shop floor, and then was up again like a rearing cobra. He still had arms, long and thin with longer, thinner fingers, but he couldn't be called human.

No. This isn't happening. It can't be.

But it was. The thin man was getting thinner, longer, trailing back the way he had come, and his limbs now had other slender growths ending in hooks. His skin was yellow and scaly—fishlike—and his eyes were hard, black, and shining like buttons. His spindly limbs were still lengthening, and his mouth was becoming snout-like, long and narrow like one of those ancient, fish-eating crocodiles, and like them, his jaws were lined with teeth like nails.

Sea dragon.

Not exactly, but there was enough of the creature from the Smithsonian brochure about the form the man had taken to bring the name swimming to the forefront of her mind. She had seen one on a road trip to the Georgia Aquarium with her parents, and it had been a strange, ungainly beast, the seahorse's ugly and more obviously predatory cousin. The thing that had been the pawnbroker opened his long, lipless mouth and words, clumsy and furred, came out.

"Give it to me," said the monster. "You would not like me to take it."

Trina froze, stricken as if cast in concrete. Mind and body shut down, caught in something between disbelief and outrage, not just at the inhuman shape in front of her, but at the fact that it could talk. The echo of her flailing disbelief rang through her head once more:

No. This isn't happening. It can't be.

And that should have been enough to dismiss it all, to vanquish it. That was how it worked in books, wasn't it? You refused to believe in the horror, and in seeing through it, it went away.

"You're not real," she managed to gasp. "I don't believe in you. I refuse."

The sea dragon abomination seemed to hesitate, then its long crocodile jaws split, and its hard eyes brightened. It was grinning.

"Good," it slurred. "That will make things so much easier."

It moved toward her again, somehow sinuous and balanced as if gliding through water. Trina took another involuntary step back toward the door. As she did so, she saw that the other man, the heavier one, was gone, replaced by something as impossible and horrifying as the sea dragon. He was flopping out from behind the counter, massive and heavy but somehow shapeless, and she saw now that he was connected by tendrils like vines to the other, to the sea dragon, so that they were not two people but one single monstrous organism. As she watched, the tendrils thickened into ropes of muscle covered with the wrinkled skin of an elephant, spotted underneath with red and white pulsing suckers.

Tentacles.

Any vestige of the man he had been was gone, but the great octopus arms had already spilled out over the counter, lengthening as they did so, and now sprawled, glistening, between her and the door. In the process, they dislodged a blue, plastic egg that had been sitting on the glass top, sending it spinning across the room.

Her eyes wide, Trina fought for a grip on what was happening. None of this could be, but it wasn't stopping. She wasn't waking from the nightmare. Dimly, with terrible reluctance, she saw that the only thing left for her was to act as if it were real. Maybe if she saw the nightmare through to its end…

Trina stepped to the side, and her heightened senses scanned the racks of merchandise, passing over the switchblades and folding knives, settling on a long Bowie knife with a curved lower edge that swept up to a point. She punched her hand through the glass without a moment's hesitation, seized the knife, and brought it sweeping in a wide arc around her, slashing at one of the sea-dragon-croc-odile's limbs.

The monster almost laughed at her pitiful assault, but it couldn't conceal the way it winced away from another lunge of the knife. As before, the blade felt like a part of her, an extension of her body, perfectly balanced and obedient to her will. The creature was huge now, almost filling the little shop, and she sensed its squid-like arms behind her back. Trina side stepped, turned, and kicked hard and high at the closest squirming tentacle, narrowly avoiding another that she hadn't seen as it snatched at her. It felt hard and rubbery, and though the kick had blocked its attack, she knew she had done it no damage. The creature lashed out more tentacles, like whips. She dodged and parried, but one reached her knife hand. In the blink of an eye, it laced around her wrist and squeezed. Another coiled around her thigh and turned her back toward the open, sea dragon jaws.

Trina fought it, but it was just too strong, and between the crocodile jaws and the curling tentacles, it had her surrounded. Some primal instinct took over. Instead of straining to get away, she rolled into the creature's deadly embrace and dropped into a crouch. For a split second, the monster's wet eyes widened, losing her in the chaos, and the tentacles that had been looping around her stiffened as if confused. From down low she could see the roots of its limbs. As the pressure on her knife hand slackened, she seized the opportunity. Trina stuck the point of the blade into the exposed underside and ripped a bright green gash open along one of the octopus-beast's writhing arms.

The monster let out a bellow of pain and fury that made

the walls shake, but the tremor that ran through the coiled mass of solid muscle wrenched the knife from her hand. Her fingers snatched at it, but it was torn away from her with unmatchable force, and she did the only thing left to her. Staying low to the ground, Trina slid away from the monster's coils, scrabbling on her belly. The creature whipped in on itself, its tentacles lashing wildly, and though she saw flecks of an oily slime she took to be blood, she knew that all she had really done was make it angry.

The door was still blocked by the trailing, searching arms of the monster. Trina slithered toward the racks of hammers and power tools, getting first onto all fours, then just about upright. The thing came after her, spitting and snapping its crocodile maw at her. Half blind with terror, Trina threw herself behind the tool displays, realizing too late that she should have grabbed something off the rack to use as a weapon. She wriggled into place, eyes flashing over the pans and other random kitchenware, desperate for a knife. There was nothing, and while the creature was too big to squeeze in after her, it could certainly snake a few tentacles in. Or just brush the displays aside and bring its whole bulk crashing in on her. It was certainly strong enough. In the meantime, her refuge was as good as a cell. She risked a glance behind her, but there was no convenient back door, no broad window, nowhere to go.

Apparently satisfied that it had her trapped, the creature seemed to gather itself, considering its final onslaught. It watched her with its beady black eyes through the gap between the displays, weaving and undulating as if in an unseen current, and suddenly its dreadful face looked less like a crocodile and more like a bird, a bird with a long, cruel beak suitable to stabbing precisely...

The thing from her dream, disguised somehow, but somehow, definitely the same.

Trina felt the fight drain out of her. She was defenseless, pinned in place by a creature from her nightmares...

And then the bell over the door tinkled. The monster's head whirled around to see who had come in. It issued a long, menacing gasp, and its eyes met hers again, held them for a breathless, considering second, and then whipped away.

It roared its vengeful malice as it turned on whoever—or whatever—had blundered into the shop, and Trina could stand it no longer. She forced herself out of her hiding place, hardly daring to look at the fight on the other side of the little shop. From behind, the monster was a boiling mass of tentacles, striking like cobras and squeezing like pythons, and above it all, the great, impossible bird head with its needle-sharp beak screamed its wordless rage. A hand shot up from the heart of the monster's attack, a human hand.

A child's hand.

It opened wide, fingers splayed like an exclamation of shock and disbelief, of pain. For a moment, the gesture was sharp as if each sinew of each digit was trying to pull itself away, the wrist and fingers hyperextending. Then the stiffness was gone. The hand crumpled and fell into the squirming horror that surrounded it, and Trina knew that there was nothing she could do to help, even if she had the courage or means to do so.

She had neither. She had only terror and despair, both of which threatened to overwhelm her.

But she also had the merest sliver of time. The creature's murderous focus was on whoever had just come in, and the tentacles by the door had gone quiet and still, as if forgotten by the bird-headed sea dragon in its feeding frenzy.

Trina took two long strides and hopped the first tentacle where it lay. The second seemed to wake up as she landed, its suckered length flexing, its tip probing the air where she had just been, and over her shoulder she sensed the bird thing turning toward her. She flung herself at the door, sobbing in revulsion and despair as she felt another tentacle brush her thigh.

Brush, but not catch.

Another leaping stride and she thundered into the door so hard she was sure it would shatter, and then she was out and running as she had never run before. She had gone two blocks before she risked a look back, but there was nothing coming after her, nothing, in fact, to suggest that anything out of the ordinary had happened.

Trina stumbled toward home, tired beyond measure and utterly bemused. Her arms and legs trembled, actually *shook*, and her first steps were tentative, as if her knees might fold beneath her when she put weight on them. Even with her new heightened senses, her new poise and balance, she had been made clumsy by shock and exhaustion so that she felt more like her old self. It wasn't an encouraging feeling. She leaned against the Eighth Street café with its whimsical chalk board of menu items and jokey invitations, which was as close to hipster chic as Treysville could muster, and fought the urge to throw up. Realizing that the aroma of coffee and hot chocolate wasn't helping, she shoved herself upright and took five careful steps, shedding a little of her unsteadiness with each.

All along Main Street she walked, wishing she still clutched the Bowie knife beneath her torn jacket, walking briskly, hoping she wouldn't see anyone she recognized and listening for sirens. The monster in the pawnshop had looked like men when she went in; was it possible that they would file a report that would bring the police to her door? It seemed unlikely, but then she had no yardstick to measure a

world such as the one she had just discovered. And maybe—
and this was surely more likely—the world was the same as it
always had been but there was something wrong with her.
Perhaps in her madness she had done something crazy,
something horrendous. The two men in the pawnshop had
become one monster, and she had certainly hurt it. Or them.
Maybe fatally. And there had been at least one more,
someone who had wandered into her fight and...

She thought of the hand she had glimpsed, when it had
gone from rigid to slack, and she felt sure she knew what
that meant, even if she didn't understand who the hand
belonged to or what had attacked him.

Him, she thought. Yes. A boy.

And she had run away. She'd felt sure she couldn't help,
but she also hadn't tried. She'd just fled. Did that make her
guilty? Did that make *her* the monster?

She picked up the pace, forcing herself not to think of

the hand, fingers splayed, rigid

the fight in the shop, pushing away the possibility that she
was delusional, but the alternative, that the world really had
changed, that it was full of horrors draped in human form,
was almost worse. Had it always been here, this place of
magic and supernatural creatures, or had it just come into
being, triggered by something she didn't understand? She
had walked past that store a thousand times. Had the men
inside always been the things she had fought? And if things
had changed, had it affected other people? Were Jasmine and
Candace secretly experiencing peculiar abnormalities of
their own? Had they too found the world suddenly peopled
with monsters? Or was it just her who had new gifts, new
insights into the profound strangeness of the universe?

She was glad to find that her dad wasn't home from work
and she could go up to her room and close the door behind
her. For a long moment she sat on her bed, focusing on her

own breathing and listening to the silence of the house, then she snatched her phone from her backpack and pulled up a series of local news sites. Surely there would be word of the fight at the pawnshop.

Nothing.

She clicked on the little flat-screen TV she used for watching movies and scanned through the local stations, looking for earnest reporters and strobing blue lights illuminating the familiar shop fronts of Main Street.

Still nothing.

It made no sense. It had been almost an hour. A customer would have been in by now, found the carnage, and called the police. That they hadn't suggested...what? That the whole thing had been in her head? Or that something more deeply strange was at work?

She considered the phone's unhelpful findings once more, then called Jasmine.

Her friend answered on the third ring.

"Hey, girl," she said. She sounded the same as ever. Casual. Unfreaked. Trina regrouped.

"Whatya up to?" she asked lightly.

"Reading this darn Shakespeare," said Jasmine. "I don't get it. I mean, why is Miss Perkins having us read just part one of this *Henry the Fourth* thing? How will we know what happens if we only read half the story? And it's not even like part one is the start. I read some of the introduction, and it's all about this other play about a King who came before Henry."

"Yeah," agreed Trina. "It's pretty confusing."

"And then it's all these names! People named after places or the other way around. Half the time I can't tell. Northumberland and Lancaster and Westmoreland, and I'm, like, *what? Who?* And they don't even stick to the same name for each person! There's Prince Henry who they call Hal or

41

Harry, and Hotspur who they call Percy. I'm Cliff-Noting the heck out of this."

"She usually does *Romeo and Juliet*," said Trina into the phone, still marking time as if her breath were held. Jasmine sounded the same as ever, and her voice was soothing, restoring, but Trina couldn't let her guard down just yet. "I don't know why she switched to *Henry the Fourth*."

"I already read *Romeo and Juliet*! That would have been so much easier."

"Maybe that's why she switched," said Trina.

"That's cold," said Jasmine. "I mean, aren't our lives hard enough?"

"About that," said Trina. She felt like she was wrenching a door open with a crowbar, but she couldn't wait any longer. "Everything going okay with you? Everything, you know, *normal*?"

There was a brief pause, then Jasmine's voice came back, clear and guileless.

"How do you mean? I mean, yeah, so far as I know. Why? Something going on?"

It was Trina's turn to hesitate. She had always told her friend everything. Once she might have run to Candace first, even to her father, but these days it wasn't even a contest: Jasmine was her confessor. But this? How could she begin to explain? She couldn't, not now. Maybe later when Trina was clearer on what was real and what wasn't, but that conversation wouldn't happen over the phone. She squeezed her eyes shut for a second, then said, "Speaking of Percy. What's the deal with this new boy? He started talking to me in the library."

"The rude kid in the glasses who transferred from Charlotte?"

"No, the other one. Percy."

"Percy? Unless he's the Shakespeare guy, I don't know him. When did he arrive?"

"Today, I thought," said Trina, suddenly unsure.

"I haven't heard anything," said Jasmine, slightly put out that she hadn't picked up on this fairly important bit of school gossip. "I'll ask around. But spill: what's he like?"

"Not sure," said Trina honestly. "A bit odd."

"Hello? Adolescent boy!" said Jasmine in mock astonishment.

"Yeah, really," Trina agreed.

"What's a factor?" said Jasmine suddenly.

"A what?"

"A factor, it's in the Shakespeare."

"I don't know," said Trina, wanting to take the conversation back to Percy.

"It's Act three, Scene two," said Jasmine, "when the prince is telling his dad that he's going to beat Hotspur in the long run even though Hotspur seems way more impressive and a better fighter or whatever. *Percy is but my factor, good my lord, to engross up glorious deeds on my behalf.*"

"I think it means, like, an agent," said Trina, fishing in her backpack and pulling out the book. She thumbed through the pages wondering why on earth they were talking about Shakespeare. "Yeah, it means someone who works for him," she said on scanning the footnotes. "Hal is saying that all the battles Hotspur is winning will just make Hal look even better, because in the end, he'll beat him. It's the bit we were up to in class:

I will redeem all this on Percy's head
And in the closing of some glorious day
Be bold to tell you that I am your son;
When I will wear a garment all of blood
And stain my favors in a bloody mask,
Which, wash'd away, shall scour my shame with it."

Trina liked the sound of the words, and for a moment, all her other concerns went away.

"Damn," said Jasmine. "That's hardcore."

Trina grinned.

"I gotta dash," she said. "Dad just got home, and we're doing one of our daddy-daughter things," she said, making sure Jasmine could hear the eye-roll.

"Hang in there," said Jasmine. "If you need out, text me and I'll deliver a suitable emergency."

"Deal."

Trina hung up and sat on the edge of the bed, looking at nothing. Jasmine was Jasmine, same as ever. Her part of the world was utterly normal. Which left Trina where exactly? All her former questions began jostling for attention in her head once more. There was only one person who might be able to help her frame some answers, one person who seemed to think that what she was experiencing was right and to be expected. She had to find Percy.

Percy is but my factor, she thought vaguely. And suddenly a different sense of the word struck her. Factor, like factory. The place where something gets made. For better or worse, Prince Hal was made by Hotspur because dealing with him made him the man he was. Was Percy somehow making—or remaking—her?

The doorbell rang.

Trina ran, vaulting easily, gracefully down the stairs, pausing only for a fraction of a second as she put her hand to the door latch. She felt sure who would be on the other side.

It wasn't the police, a possibility that occurred to her only as she got the door half open. It was Percy.

He looked, if anything, worse than before, tired, his eyes bloodshot. The wound in his belly had soaked through his shirt, though it looked wet rather than bloody.

"We need to get you to a doctor!" Trina exclaimed.

"There's no time," said Percy, "and they couldn't help anyway. We need to get somewhere safe. Now."

"Now?" said Trina, balanced on the balls of her feet, still in the doorway.

"They are coming."

Only then did his eyes fall to the carving knife she had picked up in the kitchen without thinking.

Good thing it's not the cops, she thought.

"Oh," she said, acknowledging his glance at the long blade. She managed a half smile. "Too much?"

"Not enough," he said. "But for now, it will have to do."

4

S he told him about the pawnshop incident, and he nodded thoughtfully.

"Yes," he said. "I should have warned you. What you are carrying is precious. Other people will want it, and some of them…"

"Aren't actually people?" Trina prompted.

"Right," he said.

It was simple, direct, and delivered as if they were discussing the high school basketball game. It immediately made her feel better, more certain. Madness wasn't something you shared with someone else. Either they were both crazy or the world was. Percy seemed sane and sober, and that meant she was too. It wasn't conclusive, but it would do for now, and that thought filled her with a sense of sudden and complete relief.

"So where are we going?" she said.

They had left the house at a brisk walk, her half a step behind him.

"Out of town."

"What?" said Trina, stuttering to a halt. "I can't just take off! My dad…"

"Not far," said Percy, shooting her a quick look but still walking. "Just to the Stonehill caverns."

The caverns were a network of little caves in the hills just north of town. They weren't grand enough to be a tourist attraction and mostly got used at night by kids drinking and smoking weed.

"For someone who just arrived, you know this town pretty well," said Trina.

"I knew this was coming," he replied darkly. "I did my homework."

"And what is *this*, exactly?" Trina demanded, going after him.

"Can we just walk?" he said, brusque to the point of rudeness. "I'll tell you when we get to the caves."

"No!" said Trina, stopping hard this time and standing there, hands on her hips. "This is all…insane. It's weird and terrifying, and I need to know what's going on!"

Percy glanced frantically about as if afraid they would be overheard, but the street of little houses with their garages and chain-link fences was quiet.

"We don't have time…" he began, but she shut him down. "Make time."

He glowered at her, his jaws set and his eyes flashing, but then he sucked in a breath of air and nodded.

"The chapel on Kay then," he said. "We can be there in two minutes. It's not as safe as the caves, but I can tell you most of it there."

He watched her, and eventually she nodded.

"Then we go to the caves as fast as we can," he said. "Right?"

"Depends what you have to say," she replied.

T he church was a tiny clapboard thing, a chapel really, half fallen down and long since abandoned by its parishioners for the grand, wheel-shaped edifice with the central spire on South Albany. The Kay Street episcopal chapel—originally known as St. George's—had a stone foundation, but its roof was full of holes, and part of its east wall had crumbled away. There had been a two-story tower, which had been struck by lightning a few years ago and partly burned. Now it was ringed with sectional fencing and studded with KEEP OUT signs.

"How are we supposed to get in?" said Trina. The fencing was chained in place and heavily padlocked.

Percy glanced around furtively, then crossed the side street to the rear of the lot where a heavy cedar had grown up out of the fractured concrete, crowding the little church. At its heavily shaded foot, the wire of the fence was bent and puckered. Beneath it, the weedy grass was worn to nothing, and the hard clay had been polished by use.

"You want me to crawl through that?" said Trina.

"It's not hard," said Percy, dropping into a squat and looking around before stretching onto his belly. He winced as he did so, but dragged himself through. "Foxes use it," he said, and immediately she could smell their musk and urine, "but we'll be safe inside for a while."

He didn't wait for her, moving quickly to the chapel's side door and shouldering it open. It juddered. The church looked dark inside, but Trina suddenly didn't want to be outside alone. She sat down, then sprawled forward as if diving into a pool, and wriggled under the fence, thrilling at the sense of doing something dangerous and forbidden. Percy held the door for her, but as soon as she got inside, he closed it.

Despite the holes in the roof, the chapel was dim. The damp air was redolent with the sweet and sour scent of decay, which was more than just rotten wood. There was an animal rancidness in the dark, and Trina wondered if the place had become a nest for the foxes or raccoons that had worn the ground under the fence smooth.

She looked around in amazement. The chapel had been here all her life, had been abandoned for most of that time, but she had never been inside before, nor ever heard anything about it that would make it remarkable. She had assumed it would be like the little Baptist meeting houses dotted around the area: a few benches and a step up at one end for preaching—a plain, unornamented space without the mystery and grandeur of churches in Europe. This was not what she had expected at all.

It felt larger inside, and where she had expected pine floorboards, she was standing on stone tile. Stone also formed the ornate, fluted columns up to the buttressed ceiling, and the tracery for several stained-glass windows that sent shafts of deep blue and green light into the nave. There was a great mosaic of a lion rampant on the floor. The stone looked ancient, cracked, and rounded by centuries, which was impossible, and the whole place was shrouded with creeping vines and tangles of roots. If they had been trekking through a jungle and found some long-lost crusader chapel in a clearing, this—Trina thought—was what it would look and feel like. That it should be ignored and sitting in the heart of Treysville was almost inconceivable, but Trina's overwhelming sensation was one of peace. Dingy and old fashioned it may be, but the chapel made her feel safe, and that was what she needed right now.

Percy had moved into the sanctuary, the curved walls of which held spiderwebbed effigies of men in armor, but he was watching her and seemed unsurprised by the building's remarkable interior. Behind him, as if presiding over the church, was the statue of a saint with one of those spears with a cross guard behind the head, designed so that it doesn't slide all the way through its victim. The saint stood astride a serpentine dragon. Trina leaned on a stone baptismal font and spoke at last, her voice hushed, reverent.

"This is incredible," she said.

"It's a place of power," he answered, his voice deep and resonant in the low light. "It's why we are safe here."

"Like a sanctuary thing?" she answered vaguely. "A protected space?"

"Some things cannot reach us here," he said. "Others can if they try hard enough."

"And the one you spoke of before, the bird-headed monster thing?" she asked, not really wanting to know.

"These walls will offer no protection against him."

"Why?" said Trina.

"I said," he replied, his impatience returning. "Because he has the staff and knows how to wield it. Only the caves will protect us from that and even they…"

His voice trailed off.

"What?" Trina demanded. "We're not safe there either?"

"We will be for a time. Maybe it will be enough."

"For what?" asked Trina, her voice still low, though her blood hummed in her ears.

"For you to embrace your destiny," he replied.

"Which means what?"

He came toward her then, his shoes loud on the cracked stone floor.

"Sit down," he said.

"I'm fine, thanks," she replied.

"Suit yourself," he said, shrugging before launching into his tale. "Long years ago, a warrior angel came to defend mankind from the worst of the world's evils."

Trina frowned, poised to scoff, make some smart remark about what kind of a job she thought it was doing given the state of the planet, but something in his manner or the air of the abandoned chapel kept her silent.

"It's still here," he said. "The warrior angel chooses one person and bonds with them, shares their soul, and gives them powers. The mark of its favor is a silver sword with an impossible gem in its hilt."

He stopped speaking, but he was standing in one of the uneven shafts of light from the stained glass, and she could see his face, his eyes fixed on her. For a long moment, neither of them spoke. He was, she thought, waiting for her response, her disbelief, her mockery, and it was partly to foil that expectation that she said simply, "What powers?"

He smiled at that, a small, wry smile that said she had surprised him.

"I suspect you know some of them," he said. "It's no accident that you chose that knife, though there are finer, more remarkable blades than that, which would fit your hand better. To face the enemy himself, you will need, shall we say, an upgrade, weapon-wise. But yes, your skill with the blade, your sensory awareness, your dexterity and strength: all these come from the warrior angel. As is your immunity to the enemy's most deadly weapon."

"The staff of power?"

"Yes. To everyone else, the staff is lethal. You are impervious." He gave her a level, considering look, and she swallowed. "This is why you, and only you, can face him. When you are ready."

"And how do I get ready?" asked Trina, trying to sound determined, ready, not terrified, overwhelmed, and full of doubt, though that was what she was feeling.

"Training," he said.

"And an upgrade to my weapon?"

"Yes, though that is a quest in its own right, and we cannot yet attempt it."

"A quest? Where to?"

"I'm not sure," he said. "Though I think you should start at the Kitchener estate."

Trina made a face.

"That's been deserted for decades," she said.

Percy nodded.

"But some of its secrets have lain undisturbed," he said. "Still, we'll cross that bridge when we come to it. For now, you have to prepare yourself mentally for what is to come."

Trina thought about all this.

"You're saying I was selected by an angel?" she said, unable to bite back the edge of skepticism in her voice.

"I am. It has bonded to you. Do you not feel its presence?"

"I feel... I don't know. Different. Special. Gifted. But I don't feel like there's someone else in my head with me."

"That is as it should be. You are still yourself. It's why it chose you."

Trina frowned. For all the other preposterous things he had told her, it was this that seemed hardest to believe.

"Why me? I'm...ordinary. Less than ordinary. I'm clumsy and shy, and I have no physical talents of any kind and..."

"You have got used to thinking so," he replied, almost kindly. "But the angel amplifies what is already there. It chose you; therefore, you are worthy of being chosen."

Trina looked down, her hands tracing the stone rim of the font.

"And this just happened now because, what? I'm needed?" she asked. "Because this...this thing is coming here now?"

"Yes," Percy replied. "People are going to die, and you have to stop it."

"Here," she said, pushing for something close to irony so

that she wouldn't have to think about that *people are going to die* part.

"Yes."

"In Treysville?" she said.

"Yes."

"Treysville, North Carolina?" she said, and her tone was higher now, just this side of a laugh.

"Places of power are not always recognized by ordinary people," he replied. "Take this building. You have passed it a hundred times without wondering what was inside. As for Treysville, I'm afraid the place is less important than the whim of the enemy."

"*Whim?*" Trina echoed, disbelief and annoyance making her louder than she had meant. "You're saying this big bad is going to attack here just because it feels like it?"

"Yes."

"I don't understand."

"Neither does anyone else," said Percy, his tone rising to match hers. "Evil is arbitrary. It's indiscriminate. That's part of what makes it evil."

"Okay," said Trina, raising her hands and splaying her fingers. "Okay. Say you're right…"

"I am."

"I said *say you're right*," she shot back. "Don't argue! I'm trying to understand this." She let the phrase hang between them, and he nodded into the silence.

"I'm sorry," he said. "Go on."

"So, tell me about this enemy. Who is he? Where does he come from?"

"It's not a he," said Percy. "Or if it was once, that part of him is long gone. I don't know what made him what he is, and at this point, I cannot afford to care. We call him *Anima Absentia*: the Soulless One. He's a monster, and he does what monsters do."

"But what does he want? Maybe there's a way to reason with him…"

"There's not. What he wants is to destroy, to devour the world. He delights in terror and carnage, the more, the better. I need you to listen to me, Trina," he said, stepping close enough to touch and giving her a level stare. "Do not try to talk to him, to reason with him. Do not show him pity or mercy, for he will show you none, and the attempt on your part will only make you vulnerable. He comes here to kill. That is all. And he will target you above all others. He wants you, and he will destroy anyone who helps you, anyone in whom you confide…"

Trina stared back, and her hands went to the chain about her neck.

"Because of this?" she said, her fear spreading like wildfire through her mind.

"Yes. He wants power over the warrior angel within you. But he must never get it, for then his power for evil would be limitless."

"Then I should leave!" said Trina. "Get out of here. I can save Treysville by going away, and if he comes after me, I can keep moving…"

"For how long? A week? A year? Ten? He will never stop, and he could find you at any time. You must face him, Trina. You cannot avoid him forever."

"Maybe I could stay here," she said, taking in the dappled light of the old chapel. "This feels safe enough."

The words were barely out of her mouth when there was a low rumble that seemed to come from all around them. The very ground trembled under their feet. Dust and stone chippings fell from the fractured roof and the apse above the altar.

"What was that?" said Trina as the vibrations subsided. "Just a passing truck or…"

"No," snapped Percy, wheeling about, his eyes wide. "He's here. Look."

But at first, Trina could see nothing. The air was still full of the haze of powdered stone and ancient, worm-eaten wood. The motes swirled in the patches of sunlight like smoke, but there was no sign of an intruder. The door they had come through was still closed, and the one at the front was heavily barred.

"There!" said Percy, pointing up to the altar.

Through the dusty fog, Trina could make out four man-sized shapes, evenly spaced, moving stiffly, descending… It took her a moment to realize that they were the stone knights whose effigies had guarded the apse of the chapel. They wore full plate armor including closed helms with only slits for their eyes, and they brandished long swords.

They stepped through the thick air, and as the light fell on them, Trina could see that they were, so far as she could tell, still stone, still draped with cobwebs. Their movement was slow but implacable, and it was clear where their attention was focused.

"What do we do?" gasped Trina, taking a step back.

Percy was bent over, hunting amidst the broken pews for something he could use as a weapon.

"We fight," he said, straightening up with a length of what might have been pipe. "And then we run."

"But we were supposed to be safe here!" Trina pleaded. "I felt safe here."

"This is what he does," said Percy, bracing himself as the first of the knights came almost within striking range. "He takes the places we know and the things we trust, and turns them against us."

And then he swung the iron pipe hard. The first knight blocked his attack with his stone sword raised, and the crash of their meeting rang through the air like a great and terrible bell. Trina was so struck by the sound and the strangeness of what was happening that she was almost too late to respond as the knight nearest her—this one wearing a breastplate etched with the same lion rampant as appeared in the floor mosaic—lunged.

She dodged elegantly, thoughtlessly, but still almost fell in her rush to draw her blade. The knight's sword stabbed the air where she had been, and she brought the carving knife down hard into the long stone blade's center. Perhaps if the knight had been muscle and bone and the sword had been sprung steel, her instinctive attack would have done nothing, but both the knight's arm and his weapon were unforgivingly stiff, and the sword shattered beneath her strike. She kicked him squarely in the abdomen before he could react, and he crumpled, just as the second came stumbling into range, its own sword raised high above his head.

Coming in under the blow, Trina lunged up into the stone knight's throat. She had no idea how to kill these things, but she could render them less lethal. As the knight buckled at his knees and collapsed, she turned with a surge of triumph to see how Percy was handling the other two. He was trading blow and parry with both at once, though one was disarmed, and was hacking with the flat of its hand as if it was a cleaver. Trina crossed toward him, full of adrenaline and vengeful joy.

"Go!" he shouted, seeing her approach. "Get out while you can!"

"Not without you!"

But then she saw it out of the corner of her eye: a movement at the rear of the altar, something large and pale in the darkness. It was followed by a long, malevolent hiss. She turned as the statue of Saint George, twice her size, and armed with a ten-foot lance, stepped aside to release the dragon pinned under its foot. In art and myth, they had been enemies, but here they were united and coming for her.

The dragon's form was mostly snake. It had skinny, clawed limbs and a pair of ineffectual looking wings, but it was fast, and its open mouth revealed fangs like sabers. It came first, the statue of the saint following, his shield in front of his chest and his lance raised to strike. It was massive, seeming to fill the little chapel as soon as it leapt down from the altar, and suddenly all Trina's confidence and poise evaporated. The scale of the thing overwhelmed her, and she was her old self, awkward and frightened, as if the warrior angel had never touched her at all.

5

I can't do this!" she shouted, stumbling backward, tears in her eyes.

Percy couldn't turn from the knights he was fighting, but he shouted. "You can! You must."

Which was the simple truth. If she didn't fight, they would both die. That much was clear. But the knife in her hand, large though it had seemed when she had chosen it, now felt pathetically inadequate. She looked round to where the lion-knight had fallen and spotted his stone sword lying beside him.

It would have to do. She switched the knife to her left hand, leapt, and rolled till she reached the fallen knight and came up with the stone broadsword stretched out before her. It felt heavy, poorly balanced, but there was a kind of logic to using the weapon of a statue to fight a statue.

The dragon reared up over the benches, its wings fluttering fast, not so much flying as levitating, taking the weight off the muscle in its tail. Its great mouth was agape, its long, sinuous body pale as chalk. In her mind's eye, Trina saw Eowyn standing before the winged beast ridden by the Lord of the Nazgul, and then—suddenly full of Eowyn's composure—she was ready, waiting for the creature to commit to its attack. It lunged. Trina sidestepped, swinging the stone sword and lopping off its head at the neck. The rest of the body writhed as if plunged into boiling oil. The head skittered across the church and crashed into the wall.

Even as the dragon perished, the saint's lance stabbed down at her. She caught its cross guard on her knife and pushed it aside, but the force of the strike was immense, and she couldn't deflect it wide enough. The spear tip nicked her shoulder, tearing her shirt and opening a seam-like cut on her bicep which stung like hot metal. She cried out and ducked away, hacking wildly with the long sword and hitting nothing. The swing threw her off balance, and she fell, sprawling amongst the dusty pews as the great statue stamped down at her with one massive stone foot.

Trina rolled and crawled, like the dragon she had been fighting, gasping in the dusty air as she fought to stay a foot ahead of the stone saint. In a heartbeat or two she had reached the rear of the chapel, lying on her back under the benches, and listening for the statue's approach.

She sensed the strike a fraction of a second before it came, and rolled to her right, slamming into one of the bench's legs as the stone lance head smashed through its seat and into the flagged floor. Trina shrank away but knew that if she stayed where she was, pinned in place by the benches and fallen masonry, she would be dead in no time at all. She slithered back the way she had come, toward the great stone sandaled feet of the rampaging statue, and—with a breathless rush of wild determination—through his legs. Then she was up and cutting at the back of his thigh with the stone sword.

Her stroke scythed one leg off at the knee, but he put one massive hand down onto the back of the bench to steady himself, and turned, readying the lance like some ancient fisherman spearing a salmon. She stabbed with the knife, but the statue seized it in its big, cold hand and snapped the blade from the hilt. The shock of the thing made Trina hesitate. The statue's hand flung the broken knife away, then swung back, slapping her off balance and down. She tried to roll away as before, but it brought its remaining foot down hard on her sword arm, pinning her in place. She felt the stone sword splinter in her grasp.

Trina shrieked in pain and terror. It was over. She had lost before the true enemy had even shown himself. She stared up through tears as the statue's blank eyes gazed down on her, and the lance swung into position, its head directly over her heart. It aimed, then stabbed downward with all its force.

With a shout of exertion, she caught the lance's cross guard in her left hand and held it. The spear tip was inches from her chest. Less. The statue hesitated, surprised by her strength and agility, but now it was pressing down. She pushed back, focusing all her energy up the shaft of the spear, but the statue was too strong for her. The lance slid down another inch. Two.

She kicked wildly, but though the statue adjusted its grip, she could not make contact and her strength was failing. She could feel the point against her sternum. Another second and it would puncture her ribcage. It continued to press straight down, and she knew she couldn't fight it any longer.

So she didn't. Instead of pushing up against the force of the thrust, she pushed down, toward her feet, a single, desperate concentration of energy that pulled from her a deep roar of anger and the very last of her strength. The lance snapped at the midpoint, just below her attacker's massive fist, and the statue stumbled forward. It would fall on her and crush her where she lay. It was bound to. But then it was regaining its balance and swiveling to finish her.

In doing so, however, it had taken a hobbling step and released her arm. She snatched the fallen head of the lance and, guiding it with both hands, thrust it up into the statue's belly. The tip entered like hot steel through wax, traveling up a foot or more into the statue's thorax. The effigy arched its back in silent agony, wrenching the lance from her grasp as it twisted away, then it fell like a tower, shattering on the chapel floor.

For a moment, she just lay there, stunned, registering the silence, and then the world erupted. The chapel was full of thunder and the flickering, terrible light of explosions that sent the roof and upper windows up and out and showering back in shards and fragments.

"He's here!" shouted Percy, shoving aside some of the wrecked benches where she was sprawled on the hard, flagged floor. "We have to go. Now."

He thrust a hand toward her, and she took it. As soon as his fingers grasped her forearm, he was dragging her up, the church shattering around them. Lumps of rock, splinters of colored glass, and remnants of burning wood showered down around them like a storm from the end of the world. The noise was deafening, a drumming, pounding, merciless sound as the building reduced to rubble.

Trina staggered blindly toward the door, shouldering it aside as the church erupted in fire and ash behind them. Clutching the wound in his stomach, Percy pushed her toward the fence, his face a mask of blood and grit.

"Go!" he said. "I'll stall him."

"No!" she shot back.

"I'm safer without you," he retorted. "Go and I'll catch up."

Trina hesitated, but Percy had already gone back inside.

"*Run*," said a voice within her. It was the angel, the warrior spirit that Percy said had bound itself to her. She was sure of it. It sounded calm but certain. Urgent. And if there was any doubt, it said it again.

"Run."

She did. She ran, driven by blind, searing panic, feeling strangely naked with no weapon to hand. The knife and stone sword were broken, and the Saint George lance had broken with its owner. She knew that Percy was not with her, knew he had said he was safer without her, but she felt guilty fleeing like this after all they had been through. It was the pawnshop all over again, the hand with the splayed fingers that she couldn't—didn't—save. It felt like failure, and though she barely knew Percy, the weight of losing him hung around her neck like the necklace he had given her, weighing her down like the great stone hands of the statue she had fought. She kept moving, but she could barely see through the fog of her own tears, and with each step away from the enemy's awful thunder, her body allowed its wounds to shriek their protests.

Percy's decision to stay behind had been a tactic, a device to distract the enemy, dividing his attention so as to buy safety for one of them. Or had he gone down to the monster's weapon? Percy had told her she was impervious to it. He was not.

Trina stopped running. For all her panic, she was still only a block from the chapel. She could still go back. Hers had been a blind, instinctive sprint taking her not toward anywhere, just away, but now she turned and looked back the way she had come.

She froze in breathless horror.

Standing in front of what was left of the little church was a dreadful figure, bird-headed and malevolent. The Soulless

One. It wielded a rod of bright metal that spewed fire and lightning and tore the chapel apart. Amongst the wreckage of the burning husk, nestled among the roof spars and heaps of shaped and shattered stone, was a plastic chair with chrome legs. The creature with the long, cruel beak scanned the wreckage slowly and then rotated in her direction. At this distance it was impossible to be certain, but she felt sure its eyes were locked onto her.

There was no sign of Percy.

Trina stared, then turned and broke once more into a steady run, her eyes streaming. It no longer mattered that she was unarmed. What could she possibly use to fight the beaked creature that had levelled the church after turning its aura of comfort and security against her? Nor did it much matter where she went. She just had to go.

"Sorry," she whispered to Percy, wherever he was.

Her legs throbbed and ached. Her left ankle shot notes of pain up her calf with each step so that she was already favoring the other. In time, she suspected, her run would become a limp, warrior angel or no warrior angel. Her right arm was a dull throbbing bruise that would spread from wrist to elbow where the statue had pinned her, and her left bicep keened where the lance tip had opened a razor line down from her shoulder. It could have been much, much worse, but the pain was swelling throughout her body. Eventually it would become debilitating, and if she kept running, without pause to rest and dress her wounds or tape her ankle, that would happen sooner rather than later. Whether Percy was in worse shape, she hardly dared to speculate.

Two blocks on, she risked a glance over her shoulder and, seeing nothing out of the ordinary, gave herself permission to slow down, if only to decide where she was going. She had moved east, roughly following the line they had taken before reaching the chapel, but she was now leaving the last houses of the little town center behind her. Ahead was a weedy parking lot, an abandoned gas station, then a couple of small fields that never grew much of anything, and trees. A quarter mile farther on, the road would climb, cutting back on itself as it wound through scraggy and uneven woods, and a little farther, beyond a belt of yellow pines…

The Stonehill caves.

That was where Percy had said to go, and it was where he would try to meet up with her, assuming he had gotten out of the chapel himself. He had said they would be safe there. Trina reminded herself, redoubling her stride. She would rest when she got out of sight, in the forest if necessary, in the caves if she could make it that far without stopping. The street ahead of her, in so far as it still could be called a street here on the edge of town, was deserted. Was that strange out here? She wasn't sure, though it seemed odd that she hadn't seen a living soul since long before the chapel. Not even a car moving along the road. Maybe the world was paying attention after all. Perhaps the population of Treysville was hunkered down, glued to their TVs and phones waiting for the police or the military. Maybe that was what she should be doing.

But only she could fight the Soulless One. That was what Percy had said. Only she had the warrior angel to guide her. Only she was impervious. Right now, with her aches and cuts and bruises, she didn't feel it. But then Percy had also said she would have to train before facing the monster. She had no idea how long that would take, or whether the Soulless One would find her before she was ready, but if the caves were the safest place for her to be till that time came, that was where she was going to go.

She checked over her shoulder once more, then clambered over a fence and into a scrubby field. She had felt the urge to vault it and maintain her run, but the twinge in her ankle hissed its caution, and she played it safe. She couldn't afford to sprain it further on the uneven ground, and there might be copperheads in the long grass, so she kept her eyes down. She passed an empty, derelict-looking barn with a rusted tractor sitting out front, and made her way across to another paddock fence, which she climbed over. The dirt road there took her straight up into a stand of trees and the closest thing to cover that she'd had since leaving the church.

As soon as she was deep enough into the glade, she paused, bending at the waist and sucking in the resin-scented air. There were cigarette butts and a couple of beer cans in the pine straw, and they were as good as a signpost. She turned and saw where the undergrowth was flattened into the clay of a rough path that skirted the woods and scaled the rocky outcrop beyond. She could hear bird calls coming from the deeper part of the forest and, for a moment, it was as if the world was normal again, that she had woken from a nightmare where nothing made sense. It was only the throbbing in her arms and legs that told her that what she had survived today was real and she could not wish it away.

The path wasn't especially steep, but it was uneven: often little more than a stone burnished of grass and lichen by footsteps, or a hard clay gully through the weeds. When it rained hard in the hills, the track was probably a turbid stream, but now it was dry and compacted, almost rock hard. Trina picked her cautious way up and along, watching the woods fall away beside and below her till she turned a corner and saw, through a patchwork of branches, the town she had left spread out beneath her. A pillar of smoke rose from where the church had been and hung in a cloud over the area like poison. Like death itself.

It was ridiculous to look for a glimpse of Percy from here, but she did it anyway, rising onto her toes. Seeing no sign of him, Trina turned deliberately away and kept walking, wishing she could call Candace or, even more so, Jasmine. But Percy had told her to confide in no one because doing so would put them in harm's way. Except that they already were, along with everyone else. He had said that too.

"Evil is arbitrary. It's indiscriminate. That's part of what makes it evil."

Trina sighed, but it came out as a ragged sob laced with guilt and failure. She wanted to talk to her friends, but if there was any chance that might make the monster target them first, she would not be able to live with herself. Even, she thought, if that period was cut brutally, tragically short.

So she trudged on, painfully aware that she was slowing, but a few minutes later, she saw a fissure in the sandstone cliff, taller than she was but slit-like and dark within. For a second she just stood there, conflicted. On the one hand, the caves would be dark and she had no clue what she would find inside: on the other, Percy had said they were safe. But she had left Percy behind, and though she continued to stall, hoping that he would come jogging up the trail, berating her for not waiting, there was still no sign of him. Trina glanced around, chewing her lower lip anxiously, then she approached the opening in the rock. She took a deep breath and, turning sideways, forced herself through.

6

Once through the narrow fissure, the cave opened dramatically, and there was enough light to make out the blackened powdery remnants of campfires with their scatterings of cigarette bumps and beer cans. The cave walls were soot stained, and the floor was compacted gray ash and chippings. At the back, where the cavern tightened, there was a hole, which led to the next chamber.

How far in was she supposed to go? She had heard that there were several chambers that were fairly easily accessible, but to press deeper into the complex took more nerve than most people possessed, and parts were roped off so that you had to knowingly break the law for the thrill of risking life and limb. Trina had never been beyond the first two rooms. After those, she had heard, you had to spend a lot of time on your belly in total darkness, and there were parts where the floor fell away, opening onto deep shafts or underground rivers. From time to time people died in here, and sometimes they just went in and never came out. A few years ago, there had been a movement in the local paper to make the caves more tourist friendly, but the resultant exploratory report said that the cost of rendering even a fraction of the caves safe enough for casual visitors was far too high for Treysville's pocketbook, and the only direct consequence of the report was that more warning signs had gone up. There may be safety of a kind here for Trina, as Percy had promised, but it came with perils of its own.

In the second chamber, she faltered, and in the third, she stopped entirely. While the first had been scarred with signs of visitation, of summer nights, and even of campsites for homeless people passing through, the third, which was lower ceilinged and considerably darker, felt abandoned. There was some scrawled and illegible graffiti on one wall crudely etched with a stone or knife, but no other sign that anyone had even been there. The opening into the fourth chamber was tighter still, requiring her to climb up through what felt like a window. The space on the other side was even more cramped and completely dark. Trina felt her way around the room, head bowed low as she moved into the corners, fingers tracing the wall while her other hand was out in front of her face. It took a couple of minutes to find what seemed to be the connecting passage to the next room, and she wasn't happy about it. She circled the chamber twice more to be sure and resigned herself to the truth. Unless there was some other route via one of the earlier rooms that she had not noticed, the only way on from here was down a narrow stone chute at floor level. Even though her eyes had adjusted some to the depth of the gloom, she could not see how far it went without climbing in. In the same instant, it occurred to her that if the monster were to follow her into the caves, she would not be able to slip past him unseen.

He could already be outside, she thought. *Waiting.*

Maybe he was too big to get in and was just going to stay out there until madness and starvation forced her to return the way she had come. She felt like a mouse who'd sniffed her way into one of Jimmy-Jack's "humane" traps and now couldn't get out.

Unhelpful, she told herself, and opted to root around on the ground till she found a rock she might use as a weapon in extremis: round enough to fit her hand but with a jagged, flinty edge. She liked its heft and thought it might scare off anyone—which was to say any *ordinary* person—who happened to blunder in on her, though she knew it would be no use against the kinds of horrors she had already battled. Then she sat on the edge of the chute, feeling inside with hands and feet, trying to determine how far it went. The air smelled dry, but she couldn't determine if it was also stale. She thought of Gandalf in Moria, trying to choose between three passages.

"I have no memory of this place…"

She knew the feeling. At last, though she had been wanting to save its battery, she turned on her phone and used its light to scan the rock tube.

The light was hard and flat, making depth difficult to read, and when she adjusted it, the shadows leapt confusingly. She shut it off, then closed her eyes in the hope of recovering a little night vision. So far as she had been able to tell, the chute was only smooth for a few feet before growing craggy and turning hard into darkness. Pale, leggy insects with long antennae and translucent bodies had scurried away from the light. She almost wished she hadn't looked.

What else might live here? Rats? Perhaps. Bats, almost certainly, and while she didn't especially mind them in the abstract, she didn't like the idea of brushing into them, getting their claws tangled in her hair as she tried to squirm through a tube no wider than a coffin…

Stop it, she told herself.

She had enough to worry about without conjuring new

horrors in what was supposed to be her safe place. But then the chapel had felt safe too.

"Safe."

She spoke the word aloud in the hope that hearing it would make it true. Her voice sounded thin and hesitant.

"Safe," she repeated, stronger this time, forcing a little conviction into the syllable and then listening to the echo, bright and hard in the darkness. She held onto the sound and slid down into a half squat, her back against the cool rock of the cave wall, feeling a little better. Whatever blasting thing the Soulless One was carrying, it wouldn't reach through yards and yards of solid stone to hurt her here.

Trina checked her phone, but there was, predictably, no signal. She was alone and cut off from the world, at least until Percy arrived—assuming he was still coming—or till she decided she was ready to move on.

But to where? She settled on the rock floor beside the mouth of the chute, sitting with her back against the cave wall, and thought. Percy had mentioned the old Kitchener estate as a place where she might find a suitable weapon. The ruined mansion may still have some secrets, he had said, though whether that was wishful thinking on his part, she had no way of knowing. She frowned at the thought. There was no question that the abandoned mansion was spooky, but the idea that it might contain some kind of occult arsenal was hard to believe. Still, she told herself, she had heard rumors of something close by the old house, now that she came to think about it: an old cemetery, maybe, or some kind of ceremonial stone circle. They were probably nothing more than campfire stories, but today, she reminded herself, was not the day to question what was plausible.

As locals were fond of saying, North Carolina was the site of the first American gold rush—Cabarrus county in 1799—which was partly why its major city—Charlotte—was a financial center to this day. The Kitchener family had made a lot of money gold mining in the early nineteenth century, and the great house they built, eccentric though it was and surrounded by sprawling gardens, had been the glory of the region. It should have been something to rival the Vander-bilts' Biltmore palatial estate over in Ashville, though the Kitchener place was as odd as it was grand, not so much a stately home as a castle out of a Disney cartoon. When the family's fortunes unraveled, the house fell into disrepair, and by the time it went onto the market, it needed too much work to attract a buyer. In time, disrepair became dereliction, and the house moldered away. There was talk of converting it into a theme park, but a fire in the nineties put pay to that. Since then it had been abandoned and locked up. If Treysville hadn't been so perfectly placed miles from anywhere, a buyer might have snapped it up just for the land, but land was hardly in short supply in middle North Carolina. From time to time there were tales of break-ins, but they were mostly dares and homeless people. There hadn't been anything to steal at the Kitchener estate for decades.

But if there *was* a place close by, Trina thought, where eldritch rites had hidden away a weapon of supernatural power, a place furled in legend and avoided by the general populace, it might be that old Kitchener house. It was a realm of high stone walls with mock battlements and crenelated towers as if built to withstand an army of orcs. It would also be a maze, and a dangerously unstable one at that. She wouldn't know where to start looking, and the prospect of going alone chilled her to the core, but she could see the possibility of the house as the last resting place of the weapon she needed: a sword, surely, something with an ancient name, forged by strange beings using magical ores, its blade wreathed in old world enchantments… In spite of her weariness and fear, in spite of the pain of her battered body, in spite even of her loneliness, guilt and anxiety there in the dark, Trina smiled.

Trina was, she would be the first to say, both a nerd and a geek: diligent, studious, and bookish, but also whimsical, excitable, and passionate. So was Jasmine. They liked to say that Candace had grown away from them because she had become cooler, more popular, but they knew it was as much about the fact that Candace had never quite shared their interests in fantasy roleplaying games, sci-fi novels, paranormal TV shows and movies, even the occasional cosplay convention. Candace had joined in when they were little, but it had always been play for her, something to put away at the end of the day, something to replace with other interests as she grew up, boys not least. For Jasmine and Trina, their comic book reading and movie marathons, weren't play; they were life. They were true, and that was why Trina smiled now in the dark of the cave. Because her girlhood fantasies were happening all around her, and terrible though they may turn out to be, they were also thrilling and, in every sense, awesome.

That, she knew, was a dangerous thought. It was one thing to glory in superheroes and figures from legends: another thing entirely to step into their shoes, to gird your loins, and face the enemy in battle.

But you've already done that, she thought, thinking back over the monsters in the pawnshop, the statues in the chapel. She had bested them. Or rather she and the warrior angel within her had.

Another smile.

Trina the Impervious, defender of…

She stopped short and looked up, though there was nothing to see in the darkness of the cave. She had heard something. Just a stone, perhaps, rolling on a hard floor, but a stone set in motion by somebody. Or something. The echoes were confusing, and she had no idea where the sound had come from, or how close. Trina was not alone in the caves, and as sudden as the smile had come, it was gone, along with all her imaginings of fantasy triumph. The noise had been little more than a trickle of sound, but Trina's fear returned, thick and paralyzing as the darkness.

She kept very still, eyes wide but seeing nothing, and listening. The curious, flat echoes of the caverns amplified and distorted every sound, but the more she thought about what she had heard, the surer she was that the sound had come not from ahead but from behind her, from one of the chambers she had come through. Her heart started to thump in her chest, and with the sensation came another impression: the scent of sweat and bleach.

The sweat was not hers, but then she didn't think it was whoever had dislodged the stone either. It was the caves themselves. As to the bleach…?

The scent was there only for a moment, and then her brain was fighting for purchase on reality and pushing the delusion away. The caves smelled of nothing. There had been cinders and a little staleness when she first came in, but down here, burrowed deep into the hill side, there was no smell but damp rock. She was confused. She was imagining things. Fear was making her crazy. Maybe even the sound she thought she had heard had been nothing more than her own paranoia…

It came again, louder this time, and was followed by a second.

Footsteps. Stealthy and cautious. There could be no doubt.

Trina bit her lip and cradled the rock in her hand, round part nestled in her palm, jagged edge forward, ready…

But that was just her panic trying to make her strong.

73

What she really felt was dread: breathless, paralyzing, stomach-churning dread. The hand with the rock in it was trembling, and the vice-like grip she kept on it was mostly to stop herself from sobbing.

Quiet. Quiet. For God's sake, quiet.

The slightest sound would let him—him? it?—know that she was there.

It could be Percy, she reminded herself. But if it was, why was he being silent? He must have known her route here was faster. Why had he not come bursting in shouting her name? And if it wasn't him out there in the adjoining cave, then who was it, and what did they want, alone and quiet in the dark?

Waiting, she thought. *He's waiting. And listening.*

And then he was moving again, three purposeful steps. Getting closer. She was almost sure of it.

The terrified whine she had been holding back began to swell in her throat. She bit it back, her jaws clamped hard together, her eyes squeezed shut. She needed to get up and go.

Perhaps, she thought, she should move, risk the chute after all. That way if he came through, she might still go unseen.

But unheard? She had gotten only the merest glimpse of the crawlspace down to the next chamber. One false move and she would surely make enough noise to bring him running. She wasn't even sure she could reach the chute soundlessly. The tight little cavern may as well have been an echo chamber. The slightest shifting of weight, of getting to her feet, might be all it took.

With exquisite care, Trina bent toward her feet. Her knees were drawn up to her chest, and she flattened her chest against them and pushed the rock in her right hand into the crevice between her thighs and her belly, not letting go till she was sure it couldn't roll out.

She was wearing sneakers with laces tied in double bows. With agonizing slowness, she reached down with both hands and began to work the laces free, first her left, then her right. She tugged and eased, eased and tugged, till each knot came loose and then, listening now for any sound she might make herself as well as anything that might filter through from the last room, she pushed her fingers into the fabric around her ankles and tried to wriggle her feet noiselessly out. She dug her thumb into the back of the left shoe and gently pried her heel free. She then cupped the sole in her right hand, listening with horror to the fractional shifting of her shirt fabric as she moved, and plucked the shoe off. It came free, but did so with a soft plopping noise that froze Trina to the spot.

Motionless, she strained to hear, and for several seconds, she thought there was nothing. And then, on the very edge of hearing, a sigh…

It drifted down through the entrance to her chamber, little more than a breath but somehow inflected with the hint of a smile. Trina's fright rose like a musical crescendo, then hardened till it was a spike pressed into her brain.

He was out there. And he had heard her.

How the bird-headed monster, which had seemed so big, had gotten in, she couldn't say, but all her instincts said that it was him. Some of those instincts, she felt sure, weren't hers. They came from the warrior angel within her. Some primitive alarm in her had been touched, some ancient sensory trigger that only came to life in the presence of a predator, and it rang now like a bell.

"*Hide*," said the angel. "*Now.*"

That meant the chute. There was no time to remove her other shoe. She pushed her weight over her feet and rose in one fluid motion, but she could not mute the miniscule rustling of her clothes.

The clunk and roll of the rock.

In her rush to be gone, she had forgotten the way it nestled against her waistband, pinned in place by her thighs. She felt it slide and grabbed at it, but it was too late. Its dull thud reverberated through the cavern.

The footsteps came at once, hurried now, punctuated by another of those gasping sighs, hungry with anticipation.

Trina dived blindly for where she thought the chute was. Her aim was off by no more than an inch, but the difference cost her, jarring her shoulder hard against the stone lip and jolting her back, so she had to reach out with both hands, gauge the position of the stone pipe, and thrust herself in head first. She scrambled, remembering too late that she had left her shoe in the cave, scratching for purchase on the smooth stone, wriggling forward desperately fast, in case something should catch hold of her feet. The chute tightened like a bottle neck, and for a mad second, Trina didn't think she could get through, but then she remembered the way it dog-legged to the right. She arched her back like a gymnast and thrust herself forward, snaking round the bend. The side of the tube jutted out sharply, and she caught the back of her head hard so that everything went white, and then she was clawing for purchase, pulling herself through, but with no idea what lay ahead.

She hadn't been able to see this part in that momentary flash of her phone light, and she didn't know if the chute opened up into another cave or continued as a longer and more perilous passage. For all she knew it led to an abrupt drop that had to be navigated by rope or ladder. The only good thing was that there was no obvious sign of pursuit.

So far.

Trina fought her way through the chute, knees and elbows pushing alternately like a sidewinder, hands in front of her sightless eyes feeling for barriers or the sudden plunge into God knew what. She writhed like the insects she had seen fleeing from her phone light, a desperate and thought-less scrabble forward. And suddenly there was space around her. Getting onto her knees, she reached gingerly up for a ceiling, four feet, five feet, almost six. She hauled herself close to upright, hearing her ragged breathing bouncing back at her from the walls, spread her hands in front of her, and hobbled cautiously forward.

And then she heard the laugh. It was unmistakable, a nasty, human sound, almost a chuckle, loaded with malicious amusement. It had come from somewhere behind her, and though it was muffled by the echoes of the chute, she thought she could guess where he was and why he had laughed.

He had found her shoe.

7

I f he had found her shoe, then he was only seconds behind her. Without thinking further, Trina snatched out her phone again and fumblingly thumbed on the light. She swept it around, took in what it showed, and shut it off. She was moving before she had pocketed it.

The light had revealed a long gallery, almost a corridor. The roof height varied, but it stretched on for a good twenty yards. On the right-hand side was the cave wall, pocked with alcoves formed from stalactites and other draperies, and on the left it dropped off and opened wide into a cavern much larger than any she had seen so far. She had made out a great yellowish limestone pillar, slick with the water that had dripped it into being over hundreds of years. The path went around it, and she thought some of the ground looked filled, as if some survey team had tried to render the way safer for researchers or cavers, but she couldn't see around the column. She could move that way in the hope that it led out, or she could take a chance.

She knew of no other entrance to the caves, so the idea that the passage might lead her out seemed optimistic at best. If she went on, she would eventually have to take refuge.

Better to do it now.

She wasn't sure if that was her or the angel, but the idea came hard and clear in its certainty. She skulked on as fast as she dared, tracing her fingers lightly over the damp, cold wall to her right, probing its hollows and spaces.

The first was too shallow. The second was too obvious. The third was little more than a crack in the stone, but when she reached in, she found it opened and bent to the left, an L-shaped hollow just big enough to hide a body.

She took a steadying breath and made the choice, stepping carefully, silently in, adjusting her hips as she struggled to squeeze through.

And now she could hear him navigating the chute. She was out of time.

Trina sucked her stomach in, twisted her thorax, and drew her elbows tight to her sides, turning into the stone, grazing her cheek as she pushed her way in, inch by inch. As she did so, she heard a new sound in the chute, the shrill ring of steel on stone, the sound of a blade, and not an accidental sound: it was an announcement.

Not that she needed one. The knife itself called to her so she could almost smell the tang of its steel, feel the keenness of its edge against her thumb. But being able to sense his blade wouldn't help her so long as he was the one holding it. She might be impervious to his staff of power, but he wouldn't need that down here. Down here in the cramped darkness, a knife would do just as well, or better. And Trina was, once more, unarmed.

She was almost in, but even so, she paused and reached down, the fingers of her right hand splayed and searching. There was nothing but a pebble, no more than a couple of inches across. No kind of weapon.

But maybe...

It was a stupid, desperate ruse, a trick out of a book, but she had no other options open to her. Just before she squeezed around the corner into the hidden part of the alcove, she leaned out into the passage, drew her arm back at the elbow, and used what little leverage she could to flip the pebble forward. The throw came almost entirely from her wrist, so the moment of silence before the stone fell was a welcome surprise.

It clicked off the wall somewhere up ahead and fell into the cavern with a snickering echo. The silence that followed it was thick and lengthy. Trina didn't dare to move, even though she knew she was still visible from the passage. For what felt like an age she stayed there, straining to hear, and then the monster in the chute was moving again and she had no choice. She pulled herself fully into the alcove, turning in place like a screw driving itself as deep as it could go.

And then she waited.

For a moment there was nothing, and then there was labored breathing and the last echoing movement as he emerged from the chute. Almost immediately and horrifyingly there was light, white and hard and splashing around. A flashlight? Something like that. For a fraction of a second Trina wanted to believe it was just some caver, maybe a rescue worker come to help her out, but her brain—or the angel within it—would not let her forget the laugh or the singing of a blade dragged purposefully across stone. She didn't see how this could be the creature that had woken the statues and torched the chapel, but it was no friend.

She shrank away from the light, but the alcove was too tight. If she was visible to him from the passage, she wouldn't know till he saw her, and then it would be too late. She was stuck, unable to move, let alone resist. Suddenly her decision to hide seemed like a terrible one. And probably her last. Now there was nothing to do but wait and hope.

He was coming. At best he would pass within a couple of feet from her. At worst...

She could hear his footsteps and something else, a low whistling through his teeth, idle and tuneless. Casual. Again the light flashed around the cavern, and that, too, was careless. He had no fear of her. Why should he? The alcove still felt deeply shadowed, but if he took the time to look in, he would see her. Trina spread her palm flat to the stone. It felt smooth and glossy, like tile. She could almost convince herself that she could feel the grout lines. And there was that smell again, bleach and sweat and the fragrance of something else that was uncannily familiar: deodorant, maybe. Body spray.

The ordinariness of the aroma was so jarring, so strange, that her mind swam. If she hadn't been pressed in by the cave walls

tiles...

she might have crumpled to the ground. But then he was approaching the alcove, and the brilliance of his reflected flashlight silhouetted him briefly against the blue-white glare of the cavern: human-sized but bird-headed, the staff slung across his back, the flashlight in one hand and a long, gleaming blade in the other. She could feel it again, but while the other knives had sung to her, this felt discordant and sour. He was shuffling along, eyes forward, then turning excessively to the left and the right as if he had no peripheral vision, so that the long, cruel beak cast huge, leaping shadows around the cave. Two yards away. One.

He was there, mere inches from her head, separated only by a fold of rock. All he had to do was peer around it and she was dead.

He stopped, his beak tilting up slightly as if he was

sniffing the air. Unlike the casualness she had felt from him before, this action was deliberate, predatory.

Trina kept absolutely still, breath held. Only the pounding of her heart told her she was still alive, and that was so loud she feared he would hear it as he passed...

He didn't.

He walked on, whistling softly to himself so that she could guess how close to the yellow pillar he was. Slowly, painfully slowly, the sound diminished. Whether the flung pebble had helped, she couldn't say, but for now, he had passed on.

Her temporary victory presented a new, awful decision: she had no sense of just how far he could go beyond the limestone column, but for now, she could double back, go up the chute, through the caves, and out. How long that window would stay open, how long before he turned back, realizing he had missed her, she couldn't possibly guess.

She risked a breath. It came out uneven, trembling like the rest of her, and she fought to steady herself as the decision came into focus. She had to choose how long to wait before she snuck out. Go too soon and he'd hear her. Wait too long and he'd be back.

The rock still felt like tile, but the strangeness of that had faded as Trina's mind concentrated on the problem. She bit down on her lip, senses straining for information. The whistling was almost out of earshot. It wasn't a good index of how far away he was, but it was the best she had. Carefully she began to adjust her position, easing herself back around the angle of the fissure, millimeters at a time, turning her way out to minimize sound. That cautious unscrewing meant that, an eternity later, she emerged into the main passage backward, her face to the wall. For several long seconds, she could see nothing. If the bird-headed man had returned stealthily and was standing beside her, she wouldn't know till he struck.

She rotated her head rather than her feet, but the cave was too dark to see anything. She waited, and then there was the flash of stray light bouncing off the cavern beyond the pillar. Her heart leapt into her mouth.

He's coming back! I'm trapped.

But then the light flashed away again. It had been an accidental flick of the flashlight or whatever he was using. Not a decision heralding his return. Just a casual wave of the light.

Casual.

There was that word again. She had felt it in his whistling, even in his footsteps, which had been careful, but not especially anxious. It baffled her. How could any of this be casual? She thought back to what Percy had said about the whimsy of evil and found herself missing him in ways that were almost unreasonably painful.

But there was no time for such thoughts. She put her left hand to the wall and took her first step back to the chute, already planning how to make the ascent as silently as possible. Since she only had one shoe, her footsteps were uneven, so she had to be double careful. Once, the foot that had only a sock to protect it landed painfully on a sharp stone, which dug right into the ball, but she stifled the wince and rode out the step.

The chute felt different at this end, but this time she knew something of its bends and peculiarities, and that took away some of her terror. She practically lay on her back and eased herself in, pulling with her hands when she reached the curve, and pressing with her feet against the side. If he came back now, she would be powerless, but she couldn't think about that. Moving through the chute in this direction felt quite unlike the first time, and she could sense a difference in the air, a freshness and comparative warmth she had not noticed before. The realization almost made her laugh out loud, a wild, nervous impulse she managed to bite back. Her passage through the chute had not been soundless—that was impossible—but she thought it had been quiet enough. Even so, as she dragged herself up into the low-roofed cavern and stumbled over her own shoe, she lost the composure that had gotten her that far.

She needed to be out. To be gone. Whatever safety the caves were supposed to give her had been compromised. It was the realm of monsters now, like the chapel. That, too, was what evil did.

So, she stepped roughly into the shoe and moved quickly, too quickly to be silent, toward the exit of the chamber, and then the next, and the next, thrilling to the graying of the darkness as she approached the cave mouth. At last she was out and running, her goal suddenly clear.

Trina had survived a brush with the monster, and now she wanted nothing more than to be safe, to be in a place she knew, surrounded by her own things and the one person she knew who would fold his arms around her as he had when she was small and tell her everything was going to be all right.

Trina was going home.

8

The way back into town felt shorter this time, but then return journeys always did. Take away the uncertainty about where you were heading and everything gets easier, and that was when you weren't leaving a labyrinth haunted by a monster. Trina ran easily, tracing the descending path back the way she had come under the deep, late afternoon shade of the trees, eyes down so she didn't stumble. Perhaps that was why she did not see the barrier till she reached it.

She had emerged from the tree line beside the field on the dirt road that led back to the ruined chapel and the town center, but the road was blocked by a smoky green haze. It ascended as high as she could see and extended to right and left, seemingly forever. She could just about make out the roads and buildings on the other side, but they were shifting and indistinct, as if she had peered into a crystal ball, looking for shadows. She stared in stunned amazement and perplexity, then she approached it cautiously.

So very strange.

Trina stooped and picked up a stone, which she tossed

into the misty screen. It made no sound on impact, but dropped vertically, skipping off the ground and bouncing back toward her. Trina considered it, then, having determined that the stone looked the same as it had when she had thrown it, took another couple of steps forward. Her senses strained for any sound from the other side, but she could make out nothing. She extended her right hand and pressed it carefully into the smoke. Immediately the air seemed to thicken, getting denser with each half inch or so, until she could push no farther.

She was cut off. Or the town was. She wasn't sure which, and supposed it depended on who or what had conjured the barrier and why. It might be a defensive measure designed to protect Treysville from whatever was happening outside it, but it may just as plausibly be the opposite, a measure to stop her, the town's protector, from getting back in. If the monster was already inside, or had a way of crossing the screen, which she did not, the results might be calamitous. But the bird thing had been in the cave with her only minutes ago. It couldn't have reached the town ahead of her, could it?

"Just walk away, Warren."

Trina turned and found her three least favorite classmates glaring back at her. It was Kyle Martin who had spoken. He was the closest, standing a couple of yards behind her with his arms folded. He looked big and strong and hostile, hoping she would argue out here where there was no teacher to intervene. Steve Parks was sitting on a log to Martin's left, watching them idly, and Colin Everett was leaning up against a tree whittling a piece of wood with a penknife. Together they looked languid but poised, like wild dogs whose mood could shift in the blink of an eye. Trina had no idea how they had approached her unheard, or where they might have come from.

Even at this distance, she could feel the presence of the knife in Colin Everett's thin fingers. It wasn't especially sharp, but it worried her nonetheless, as it was intended to. With her back to the impenetrable misty wall around the town, she felt pinned, a cornered rabbit.

"What's going on?" she said, managing to sound conversational and unruffled.

"Town's cut off," said Kyle Martin. "I'd say that was pretty obvious."

"She ain't that bright," said Steve Parks. "Even Miss Perkins said that, and she's uber soft."

"She said I wasn't smart?" said Trina, stung.

"Oh what, like that's a big surprise?" said Kyle. "Or you thought she *loved* you or something?"

Steve made kissy noises and snorted with disgust.

"So gross," he said.

"She shouldn't be talking about her students is all," said Trina, knowing she sounded pathetic, wondering why in the heat of everything that had happened and was happening around her, her mind had gone to the utterly trivial concern for a teacher's attitude to her, something they were almost certainly lying about.

"Ooh," said Kyle, smirking through his mock sympathy. "We made the freako sad."

"You wish," said Trina, recovering and deciding not to be sidetracked by their nonsense.

"What are you doing here anyway?" Steve demanded, standing up and taking a couple of steps toward her.

"Trying to figure out how to get through the smoke," said Trina, glancing back at the screen. "I thought that was pretty obvious too."

"Why?" said Kyle, also moving forward, annoyed by her tone.

"Because I have to help," she replied, as if it were self-evident. "Something bad is happening."

"Yeah," said Kyle, smirking again. "We know."

"And what makes you think you can do anything about it?"

That was Colin. He had stopped his whittling abruptly and was coming over. Trina felt herself stiffen with tension, and not just because of the knife in his hands. Kyle and Steve were stupid, macho bullies, but Colin, though not as physically imposing as the other two, was something more, a different kind of cruel altogether, and she didn't like the look in his eyes.

"Someone has to," she said.

"Not you," Kyle shot back.

"Man, I hope not," said Steve. "If anything depends on you, we're all toast."

Kyle grinned at him. If they'd been at school, he might have high fived him.

And there it was again, that combination of stupidity and malice with something that was flippant, casual. It annoyed and scared her.

"No kidding," Kyle said, turning from Steve to her and giving her an appraising look loaded with scorn. "You might be the most useless person in the whole school."

"You seen her in gym?" Steve went on. "Man, it's like watching a two-legged dog." He turned to her. "You have, like, a *condition* or something?"

"I don't have time for this," said Trina. "You idiots can help, or you can get out of my way."

She said it in anger without really thinking it through. Colin looked like she had made his day. His hard little eyes lit up, and he came in close.

"And what if we don't?" he whispered silkily.

"You don't want to know," said Trina, taking one final

step backward so that she could feel the soft pressure of the smoky wall behind her. She could almost feel the blade in his hand...

"Oh, I think we wanna know, don't you guys?" said Colin, running his thumb along the edge of his knife. "I wanna know what Loser Warren thinks she can do to stop us getting in her way."

"There's something coming!" Trina tried, one last time. "It may already be here. It's going to kill people. You may be in serious danger!"

"Like I said," Kyle replied with a shrug. "We know and we don't care. In fact, we think you should leave it be."

"Yeah," said Steve. "Walk away. Go hide in the caves again."

"Yeah," Kyle agreed. "Go cry."

Trina looked away impatient and unsure what to do, but then she processed what they had just said, and she turned back to them.

"How do you know I was in the caves?" said Trina, calmer now.

"What?" said Steve, looking blank.

"You said I was in the caves," Trina replied, insistent now. "How did you know?"

"Saw you," said Steve, looking away.

"No, you didn't," she said. "And you didn't follow me down from there either. I would have seen."

"Because you are so eagle eyed?" Colin said, mocking.

"I am today," said Trina, certainty restoring her confidence. "I don't have time for you. Not today."

She started to walk away, but Steve adjusted quickly, spreading his arms so that she could not go by without a confrontation. Kyle followed suit.

"I *really* don't have time for this," she said stiffly. She wanted them to hear the note of warning in her voice, but they just grinned at each other and closed in. Any other day, she would have been scared. Now she was merely annoyed. She had to be elsewhere. She had important things to do.

Her irritation raised a question in her mind that connected with her previous uncertainty about them.

"You weren't here a few minutes ago," she said. "And then, suddenly, you were. How's that possible?"

The challenge seemed to flummox them, but she felt sure it was more than that. The glance they exchanged was instant and uniform, and for the merest glimmer of time, it was like they weren't really people at all. Trina frowned, wondering, but they were already back to their usual meathead selves.

"How's it *not* possible?" said Colin, stabbing his finger into her shoulder so hard that he pushed her against the screen.

It was as if he had made the decision for her.

"*Fight*," said the angel within her.

Trina seized his wrist before he could withdraw it, and when the other hand—the one with the knife—swept in, she grabbed that too. She held him there, and his face burned with fury and indignation inches from hers. Then his friends came lumbering to his aid and, again, the choice was taken from her.

She yanked Colin's arms to the right, lunging with her right leg so that he didn't so much trip over it as go flying with such force that he landed in a crumpled heap in the grass three yards away. Kyle came in next, his fist raised above his shoulder and his face a mask of loathing.

And in that fraction of a second, even as she calculated her block and considered the next two moves, which would render both Steve and Kyle helpless, she knew for sure that it wasn't them. They were mean for sure, but this was a different brand of malice entirely. If Kyle's punch landed, it could fracture her cheek, knock her unconscious or—if she was really unlucky—worse. And hate them though she did, that was not them. She wasn't sure who or what they were, but they were not her classmates, however they might look and sound like them.

The realization had an immediate effect, filling her with a new and necessary clarity. She raised her right hand to deflect Kyle's Captain America punch, even as she prepared to kick Steve hard in the crotch. Both actions completed, she wheeled, throwing an elbow into Kyle's face, which sent him staggering back, and closing fast on Steve, who was doubled over in agony. She thumped him hard on the back of the neck and he crumpled. As Kyle recovered sufficiently to come back at her, swinging wildly, she scythed his legs from under him with her left leg.

She followed up as he went down, her fists raised, but no coup de grace was necessary.

As he hit the ground, Kyle turned into a puff of greenish smoke like a dusted vamp on *Buffy* and was gone. Steve too. Even Colin.

Trina was alone.

As she had been since she left the caves. She was sure of that now. These hadn't been shape-shifting monsters or something sent to kill her. They had been the embodiment of her own doubts and fears, ordinary, petty even, but turned against her by something else that had reached into her head and conjured whatever was most likely to undermine her faith in herself.

It hadn't worked. She turned and considered the smoky barrier that separated her from Treysville and, just to be sure, tested it again. It was as before, soft, but finally unpassable. Wherever she was going to go next, it wasn't home. But then maybe she didn't need that kind of safety after all. Because the enemy was afraid of her. That was why it had tapped into her head to try and turn her away.

So, some other course of action was needed.

Percy had said she needed to train, to make herself ready, but there was no time for that. In the caves, Trina had been too close to death and to the thing that had casually tried to visit it upon her to wait and hope that Percy would show her the way. She had to go on the offensive, and that meant that she could be unarmed no more. She was going to the Kitchener estate, and she would choose something to aid her fight against the thing in the caves, in spite of her doubts and fear,

and guilt,

and whether she was ready or not.

9

It was almost dark by the time Trina reached the outer walls of the Kitchener estate. They were stone, some eight feet high, and though the house itself resembled a castle, these were more property line markers than they were fortifications. Tall, wrought-iron gates, chained and padlocked, stood between towering gate posts on which rusted lion statues pawed the air and roared silently into the night. Years ago, the county fair, the same one she had recently attended in a field on the west side of town with her dad, had been held on the Kitchener grounds, and Trina had gone with her parents, Jasmine, and Candace. Her father had taken a picture of them—all the girls together—shrieking with delight on the mad-eyed horses of a carousel. Trina had kept it in a silver frame on her nightstand for years. The girls—all clutching the remains of cotton candy as big as their heads—had been, maybe, eleven. Her mother looked more than happy. She had been elated. That picture had made Trina smile until a few months ago. Since her mother had died, the picture had changed, become painful, not just because it reminded Trina of good times past, but because her mother's careless pleasure now looked somehow unsuspecting, naïve, even, as if there was something stalking her that she couldn't see. It made her pitiable, oblivious to something the universe had already planned.

It made Trina blind with rage.

When she put the picture face down in a drawer a few weeks ago, her dad had asked about it. She had dodged, saying only that it made her sad. And that was true, though the whole truth was bigger and more ragged, its storm clouds packed full of fire and lightning as well as rain. Her father who was a kind and quiet man, kinder and quieter than he looked to most folks, had nodded and reminded her that it was healthy to remember the good things, and that her mother was still with them in spirit. Trina had nodded and said nothing, but she did not get the picture back out of the desk drawer where she had stowed it, and her dad didn't ask again. When she thought about the photograph now, it seemed like something from a former age, an artifact she might have unearthed on some archaeological dig, its original purpose obscure. It wasn't that she didn't remember, just that she couldn't allow herself to believe that such things had once been real. She had to focus on the present and the future: if she looked back, she feared both would unravel.

Shortly after their trip to the fair all those years ago, the estate had been sold to a developer who had closed the property to the public, and she had never been through those gates since. Now "Private Property" warning signs hung from the old ironwork, each marked with the name, number, and logo of an out-of-town real estate company. Her father said the place had been sold several times since the day of the fair, but no one had ever had the idea, or the money, to turn the grand old house into anything, and no one had lived in it since the Kitcheners themselves. Now it stood desolate, a crumbling monument to the family who had left it a century and a half before.

In spite of her determination to focus on the present, that memory of coming here with Candace years before reminded her how much she missed her old friend. Candace was an athlete, a beauty, for sure, but she was also a wit, a reader, a determined worker who stayed up all night after cheerleading to get her homework done and her tests prepared. She was a singer too, not a great one—she knew—but passionate and enthusiastic and would close her eyes in the car and belt out what was on the radio so loudly that a boy she liked once said it looked like she was on stage in front of a sold-out crowd. But that wasn't right because Candace didn't perform for other people. She sang for herself because she loved it; the music brought out in her a wild joy that freed her from all other concerns till the song finished. She became a force of nature, not a rainbow herself but a torrid river leaping over the rocks of a waterfall and crashing down with such exhilaration that she raised rainbows all around her. And then she'd blush and smile and apologize for being too noisy, for forgetting herself, though she had really done the opposite, stripped off everyone else's expectations of her and remembered who she was in her soul...

When this is done, Trina thought to herself, pushing aside any concern about what *this* was, *I'll make up with Candace, reconnect with her. Somehow.* She and Candace and Jasmine would find a carousel somewhere and recreate that photograph.

Smiling at the decision, Trina scaled the gates with ease, feeling strong and light, hoisting herself up on her toes and fingers as if she were climbing a ladder, and dropping easily to the ground on the other side. There was a long, straight but overgrown gravel road, leading through heavy, black holly trees to the house itself. She didn't know where she was going, which part of the locked and moldering structure was supposed to house the weapon she had come to find, and her greatest hope now was that Percy would be waiting for her, full of apologies and explanations for why he had not been able to join her at the caves.

And if he wasn't?

She would cross that bridge when she came to it, she decided, being deliberately glib because she could not consider the implications of his not showing up too closely. For now, she needed something positive to hold onto. It was easier to picture him stepping in front of her, his face a mask of concern and relief that she was all right as she walked swiftly, staying in the deep shadow of the trees, all senses heightened for what she may find ahead, good or bad.

The long driveway had once granted a prospect on the house itself, but at some point in the past, a copse of trees had sprouted in the cracked roadway, and a makeshift gravel track had been added to circle it so that Trina didn't see the strange fantasy castle till she was almost under the shadow of its ramparts. As she rounded the trees, it reared up ahead of her, a romantic, Gothic ruin, all unlikely turrets and towers, a deeper black against the swirling darkness of the evening sky. The last amber rays of the sunset picked out its ruined pinnacles and crenulations, making them shine, but even at this distance, she could see the blank and empty windows gazing down on her like mad eyes and wailing mouths.

The parkland of the grounds which she dimly recalled was unrecognizable. Whatever the new owners were doing, they were spending no money on upkeep, and what had once been manicured lawns were wild meadows dotted with trees and shrubs no hand had deliberately planted. Trina recalled a lake with a boat dock, but that was nowhere in sight. She thought it might be on the other side of the house, but it was just as likely that it had been drained and was now just another overgrown torrent of weeds. Ahead of her was an elaborate bronze fountain of what might have been Neptune among nymphs and dolphins, though the figures were draped in vines and some had been toppled from their bases. Other bare stone pedestals in the tall grass suggested that there had once been other statues that had been sold off or stolen. Recalling the statues in the chapel on Kay Street, and the way they had been used against her, Trina looked cautiously around. She was, after all, still unarmed.

Her visit had been intended to fix that, but she didn't know where to start looking. Even in desolation, the house looked formidably well protected, the windows on its lower stories little more than arrow slits. Any doors would surely be solid and heavily barred, and even if she could get in, she didn't know where she was supposed to go. It suddenly seemed very unlikely that she might just stumble on a secret weapon cache that had been concealed for a hundred and fifty years.

Percy, where are you?

She wanted to shout it into the night, but after her experience in the caves, she knew better than to attract attention to herself. Instead, she paced the grounds, eyes and ears open for any sign of life, and so it was that she caught distant sounds coming from the other side of the castle. There was a low thumping that her angelically enhanced senses could feel through the ground itself.

Explosions?

Trina stood very still, listening hard and in a higher register to the muffled pounding she heard…

People.

Screaming?

No.

They were laughing, whooping with that special performative delight designed to remind everyone that you were there and were having the time of your life. And now she recognized the thumping that was vibrating through the earth. It was the throbbing bass and drums of music.

Cage the Elephant, to be precise.

It made no sense, but she was sure of it. There were people singing and dancing along to "Ready to Let Go." As she broke into a faltering jog in the direction of the sound, Trina's whole body relaxed, all the tension she had not known she was carrying falling from her shoulders as if she had been wearing plate armor. She had come to the estate in dread and terror, searching for weapons, but she had found, what? A concert? No, she thought, homing in on the swelling sound and catching the first glimpse of lighted windows on the north side of the mansion; it was simpler and less focused than that.

A party!

And in spite of everything, Trina laughed aloud with relief.

The castle looked utterly different from this side, less dour and decrepit, less menacing. The structure was more clearly a house—albeit a massive and whimsical one—and less a fortress, but what really made the difference was the amber glow in the huge bay windows, the wide-open doors that spilled joy and exuberance down the formal steps to the lawn. Trina picked up speed, baffled still, but so elated at this picture of life and happiness after all she had been through that she ran on, up and in, without a second's hesitation.

The marble flagged lobby was cavernous. It was hung with fine tapestries and bright with light from a massive crystal chandelier. There was, amazingly, no trace of the rundown abandonment she had seen on the other side and in the grounds. This looked not just maintained but lived in.

"Good evening, miss," said a boy in a tuxedo standing at a

lectern on which sat an iPad. Behind him was a red, velvet rope looped across a flight of four stairs leading to an immense ballroom full of people dressed as if for a gala.

Or prom.

Yes. That was it. Because now that she looked, Trina started recognizing people, students from school, all dressed to the nines. There was Jennifer Sanchez teetering on three-inch heels, and Marty Smith, looking like a spotty James Bond. There was…

Candace!

Trina's heart leapt, and she started to wave to her friend, but the boy in the tux stepped into her line of vision. He was smiling politely, but he would not be ignored.

"I'm sorry, miss," he said, brandishing the iPad. "Are you on the guest list?"

And only now did she recognize him in his finery. It was the blank-eyed boy in gold-rimmed glasses she had seen in school but didn't know. They had bickered because he had said she was in his way. She had called him rude. There was no trace of malice in his face now, no sign that he even remembered their previous encounter, but Trina felt awkward anyway.

"Guest list?" she echoed, stupidly.

"Guest list," he replied. "What's your name?"

"Trina," said Trina, playing dumb. "Trina Warren."

Since she had had no idea the party was happening, she would clearly not be on his list, but perhaps she could feign surprise, say there'd been a mistake. Maybe Candace would help her get in.

Maybe.

The boy scanned the iPad, scrolled a little, then looked up, smiling, and moved to the velvet rope, which he unhooked deftly with one hand.

"Welcome, Miss Warren. Please take a gift bag on your way in."

Trina stared at him, unable to believe her luck, then swept on inside, the hem of her gown trailing behind her, like she was a duchess or a movie star.

The gift bags were sparkly, dainty things, light as feathers.

"What's in them?" she asked.

"Most have corsages," said the boy. "Check."

She peered in and produced a sky-blue plastic egg, about the size of a chicken's. She gave the boy a bewildered look, but his face lit up.

"Oh, well done!" he said. "That *is* unusual. You won't need a corsage with that. But don't open it. Not till the very end."

"Okay," said Trina. "Can I go in now?"

"Absolutely," said the boy. "Have a fantastic time. I'll see you later."

He gave her one more expansive smile, though it didn't quite reach his oddly empty eyes, and nodded toward the ballroom. As soon as she crossed the rope line, he re-hooked the barrier and returned to his station.

"Listen," she said, turning back to him so that he stooped, surprised, and gave her an expectant look. "I'm sorry about the other day. Outside the hall? You were going in and, well, we argued."

He smiled again.

"Think nothing of it," he said. "I'm sorry too."

That should have been enough, the closure she had needed, but Trina still felt a little off balance. Maybe it was the blankness of his eyes. She wanted to feel forgiven but...

"Go on in," he said encouragingly. "Things are about to start."

Trina nodded and smiled and decided to say no more. Instead, she turned and drifted into the great hall, marveling at the vast mirrors on the walls, which ran all the way up to the elaborately painted ceiling, depicting the knights of the round table and with a heraldic lion in each corner like those on the gates outside. It was spectacular. But it was also fun. The elegant sophistication of the place was playfully undercut by the pounding dance music, just as the haute couture clothes became ironic on classmates she'd never seen out of jeans and t-shirts.

"Trina!" shouted Candace. "I didn't know you were here! Isn't this the best party?"

"I just arrived," said Trina happily. "It looks awesome. Nice orchid."

"Gift bag," said Candace, touching her corsage. "Some people got white, some got purple. I think the white would go better with my dress, but we're not supposed to trade. There's a game or contest or something later."

"It looks great," said Trina honestly. Candace looked suave and mature in her formalwear, beautiful. "Is Jasmine here?"

"Haven't seen her," said Candace. "I figured she'd come with you."

"I don't know where she is," said Trina, scanning the dance floor where Adi and Rey, who sat with her in biology, were cavorting wildly, laughing at each other. She felt a twinge of anxiety and said again, lamely, "I don't know where she is."

"She'll turn up," said Candace. "Everyone was invited. Let's get some punch."

"They were?" said Trina vaguely. "I don't remember being invited."

"Well, you're here," said Candace, shrugging and beaming. "Come on. Let's have some fun."

"Yeah," said Trina, still a little unfocussed. "Fun. Yeah."

A part of her thought there was something peculiar about the party, something very slightly off, but the pleasure of seeing Candace again, of being received so warmly back into a friendship she thought was dead or dying, wiped all concerns from her mind.

"Have you seen Percy?" she asked.

"Percy?" said Candace, nodding to the punch bowl so that the server, a sophomore Trina recognized but didn't know, used a ladle to fill a goblet with a red liquid, on the surface of which an orange slice floated.

"Black hair, dark eyes," said Trina. "Kinda cute."

"Oh *Percival*!" said Candace, laughing. "Yeah, he's a looker all right."

"Why do you call him Percival?"

"Not sure," said Candace. "Somebody said he looked like a guy in a book they saw. A knight or something. Sir Percival."

"Like Hotspur in the Shakespeare play?" said Trina.

Candace shrugged and made a noncommittal face. "More like a round table kind of deal," she said.

"Oh," said Trina. "Right."

"But anyway, no, I haven't seen him," Candace said.

"Maybe he's ill," said Trina, fighting down the rising unease again. "He wasn't looking well earlier."

Candace shrugged again. "Oh, I love this song!" she exclaimed as the music shifted. "Let's dance!"

And they did, holding their glasses carefully away from them so as not to spill on their fancy clothes, rubbing unconsciously up against their school friends in their white and purple corsages, all rivalries temporarily shelved in the shared joy of the moment. It felt like a celebration, though if it was, Trina didn't know what was being celebrated.

She danced to two whole songs before they started that eighties thing her dad liked, the Live Aid guy singing about how he didn't like Mondays, and you couldn't dance to that. They were sitting down when, on the other side of the dance floor, she saw Percy.

Her heart leapt with gladness and relief, as the feelings she had been holding back, the guilt and anxiety and anguish, all melted away. He was okay after all. He had gotten away from the chapel in one piece and hadn't gotten stuck in the caves with the monster while looking for her. It felt as if a heavy backpack she had been wearing for days had suddenly been handed off to someone else, an almost physical reprieve.

Percy was dressed in a classy black suit and looked healthier than he had before, his eyes clearer and with no sign of the wound in his belly. He spotted her across the room, and as their eyes met, he smiled, then held her gaze and steered it upward. She followed, her eyes sweeping the imposing staircase at the far end leading to the balustraded walkway where some of the students were watching the dancers from above, and on up to where, set among a series of heraldic shields depicting stylized lions, she saw a rack of ancient weapons: pikes and halberds crossed, rows of spears, axes, maces, and, laid out as the center piece of the display, a circle of swords, their points together, their hilts radiating outward like the rays of the sun. Some were short—little more than daggers—others were great two-handed things almost as long as she was tall. There were quick, sharp rapiers and heavy, brutal-looking claymores. Now that she saw them, she sensed the way they had been calling to her, or to the angel within her, ever since she had arrived. They were straining to leave their ancient hangings and leap into her hand, shedding their merely decorative function and becoming again what they had been made to be: fine and elegant weapons of right and justice.

Trina gazed up at them enraptured, the noise and exhilaration of the party falling away as she remembered the caves, the chapel, and why she had come to the Kitchener estate in the first place. This was her mission: to find and select a weapon. She had to keep focused on that and not be seduced by the party. As she made the decision, she thought she could smell the swords, the flat tang of metal in her nostrils, though it was overlaid bewilderingly by the complex aromas of old institutional food—pizza, French fries, mac and cheese —as if they were baked into the walls of the place, so that the metal smelled less like ancient weapons and more like cheap pots and pans. She found the idea puzzling, not least because the party food was elegant little canapes and a sophisticated-looking buffet of exotic and expensive treats: nothing that would explain the oddly familiar smells.

She was still looking around wonderingly when the music stopped abruptly, replaced by a shrill, rhythmic tinkling. The boy in the tuxedo who had been policing the rope line, the boy she had quarreled with in school, was standing on the landing of the great staircase, tapping a raised glass with a teaspoon and smiling. The room fell hurriedly quiet, but the boy who was apparently function as emcee waited indulgently till the last whisper of conversation had died away before speaking.

"Welcome, East Trey High!" he announced.

There was a spontaneous eruption of applause and self-congratulatory cheering. People whooped and roared, then laughed at themselves for doing so.

"Yes," said the boy, accepting it all and smiling as before, the smile that only affected his mouth. "Welcome. I am so glad you could make this little gathering, our little haven of peace and celebration, away from all the miseries and hardships of ordinary life. It is a joy to see you all looking so beautiful."

He paused for their applause and shouted agreements and, for the first time, Trina thought there was real emotion behind the smile, though she was confused by what it was. It felt as much like sadness as it was joy, as if this were the end of something wonderful, a vacation, perhaps, after which they would not see each other for a long time. Trina glanced around, but no one else seemed to feel what she was feeling. They looked delighted, full of life and hope and energy. She wasn't sure why that worried her, and her eyes flashed back to where Percy had been, but somehow in the crowd's gathering to listen to the spectacled boy's speech, she had lost him.

"We will now move to the more structured part of the evening," the boy went on in more measured tones, adjusting his gold-rimmed glasses. "As you came in, you each received a gift bag containing a flower, a flower which I hope you are all wearing."

There were a few seconds of unspecific bustle and a hoot of equally unspecific agreement from Marcus Sanders—no surprise there—which generated a ripple of laughter. The spectacled emcee

What was that kid's name?

allowed this, too, then raised his hands in a calming motion.

"Now," he said, sweeping one hand to the right, "if those of you with the white orchids would move to this side of the hall...?" He waited for the shifting to begin, speaking loudly over the rising babble of voices again, and motioning with his other hand. "And if those of you with the purple orchid would move to the other side, we can get started."

As the crowd parted like the Red Sea in one of those old Bible epics, Trina hesitated. Candace gave her an "isn't-this-fun?" grin, eyebrows bobbing, then joined her group on the left, but Trina, who had no corsage of either color stayed where she was, all her old embarrassment and awkwardness returning. She glanced into her gift bag again, but when she put her hand on the blue plastic egg inside, the emcee boy called her by name.

"Not yet, Trina. Save that till the end."

"I don't have an orchid," she said plaintively.

"That's okay," he said. He was still smiling that not entirely convincing smile, and now that the partygoers had been split into two groups, she found something ominous in the fact that she alone was directly in front of him. Unbidden, she thought of Corvus Glaive, Thanos's noseless henchman, dividing the people of Gamora's planet...

Her unease crested into panic, and she scanned first the white side then the purple for Percy, but there was still no sign of him. Her eyes went up to the circle of swords high on the wall above the emcee, but they may as well have been in a vault miles away. She could smell them—metal and (still and strangely) old, familiar food—but she could not reach them with hand or mind. A part of her thought that with the right kind of mental focus, honed till it was sharp and powerful, she ought to be able to wrench them from the wall with her mind, send them flashing into her hand like Thor calling for his hammer or Rey magically pulling her light saber out of the snow, but she couldn't do that. No one could.

As her gaze dropped back to the emcee in search of encouragement or explanation, she saw that he was staring levelly back across the ballroom, and his smile had gone. He looked as she remembered him from school: blank, dead eyed. There was a terrible red patch in the center of his chest, and there was dark crimson fluid pooling at his feet.

"Trina," he said, looking her dead in the eye. "This is on you."

She stared, revulsion and outrage blending, but before she could say anything, he was falling, one hand upraised, fingers splayed and stretched.

Trina turned quickly and looked back across the great hall toward the entrance where the velvet rope was now the only sentinel. Above it, standing on a little balcony under which they had all passed, was a creature with the head of a great bird. It had a long, curved beak and was holding a bright metal staff in both hands over its head. She thought it was speaking the words of a spell or incantation.

To her amazement, the air above the dance floor was filling with spheres the size of volleyballs, some white, some purple. They appeared out of nothing, popping into existence and hanging there like ornaments on an invisible Christmas tree, glowing softly. A gasp of admiration rose up from the crowd, but Trina just stared with a swelling sense of foreboding as the white spheres began to move.

Each one drifted down toward one of the revelers wearing the white flower, expanding like a great bubble until it was large enough to contain a person. Which is what they proceeded to do. As the students looked on, amused and baffled, the bubbles enveloped each of those with a white corsage, pulsing with gentle radiance as they closed around them.

And now the purple spheres were moving too, but instead of expanding and drifting, they shrank and began to vibrate with a new and terrible energy. Soon they were no larger than marbles, tight and bright and smoking hot. If it was possible for a physical object with no consciousness to be evil, to want to cause harm, then these were those objects.

"Everyone get out!" Trina roared. "Now!"

But even as she said it, the bird-headed monster screamed something she did not understand, and the purple spheres started streaking down with incredible speed and precision into the crowd on the left. As they found their targets, there was a flash, a scream, and the person who had been hit crumpled. Before they hit the ground, they exploded into smoke and dust. In less time than it took for Trina to suck the air into her lungs, half the crowd on the left side of the room was just gone.

"No!" roared Trina, but chaos had already descended on the ballroom. They were all shouting and crying and running, regardless of what kind of flower they wore. In no time at all, the two carefully separated groups had become a single, stampeding mass.

It didn't seem to matter. Those in their white bubbles were immune to the passage of the projectiles that rained down like fiery purple hailstones. Those with the purple flowers could do nothing to get away. They crouched and dodged and hid behind furniture and people, but the tiny spheres seemed to track them like malevolent insects, swerving, adjusting, waiting, then streaking to their targets with awful precision.

Nothing touched Trina. She stared around her, overwhelmed by grief and horror, but she was untouched.

Impervious.

On impulse she swatted with her open hand at one of the purple projectiles, parrying it away from its target, only to see it sweep hard to the right, pivot in the air, and come swooping back in, out of her reach. It hit Niles Fairview in the back, and he vanished in a shrieking plume of dust.

"No!" Trina screamed again, outraged and overwhelmed.

Impervious but powerless.

"Please, no!" she shouted to the balcony where the bird-headed monster stared down at her. The shape of the head, its long, cruelly curved beak, reminded her of something, but she couldn't think what. "Please stop! I'll do anything!"

"What's happening? Trina?"

The voice at her elbow was anguished more than it was truly confused. It was the voice of someone asking a question not because she didn't know the answer, but because she couldn't accept the answer and wanted to be told otherwise. It was the voice of a child who desperately needed to know, against all evidence to the contrary, that everything would be fine.

It was Candace, and she was still wearing her purple orchid corsage.

No. Please, no.

Though she knew in her heart that it wouldn't help, Trina snatched the flower from her dress, tearing the fabric as she ripped it free and threw it from her, then she looked up. Burning in the air some ten feet above them was a single purple light. It hovered as if conscious, watching, oscillating in place as if timing its next action. Without taking her eyes from it, Trina stepped up to her friend and folded her arms around her as if they were slow dancing.

"Trina?" Candace whispered.

"Shh," said Trina. "Come with me."

She took a step back toward the entrance, toward the bird-monster she couldn't see, her eyes still locked on the purple sphere above them. It matched their movement, surging from side to side, gauging its opportunity like an owl bobbing its head to get the most precise visual lock on its target.

"I'm scared, Trina."

"I know. We all are."

All around them people were running and screaming. The bursts of light and dust as people vanished were fewer now, but only because most of those with the purple flower had already gone. Many of those who were screaming were safe in their white bubbles, though that didn't make their pain at watching the deaths of their friends any less. Their faces were drained of color, their weeping eyes mad and staring, their mouths frozen.

Deaths. The deaths of their friends.

There was no doubt in Trina's mind that that was what she was seeing. It wasn't like when she had fought Kyle and

Steve and Colin and they had disappeared. They hadn't really been there. These were. They were flesh and blood, spirit and thought and feeling, or they had been. Trina could feel their lives winking out of existence like so many snuffed candles.

She kept directing Candace in their clumsy, retreating waltz, still watching overhead. Once, it dipped toward them and Trina threw up the flat of her hand like Ironman directing a blast of energy. The sphere retreated, hesitated, and then divided.

Into two.

Then four.

Then eight.

The lights buzzed about, adjusting like a squadron of aircraft or a tiny purple swarm of wasps.

"No!" Trina yelled. "That's not fair!"

She heard the petulant inadequacy of her words bouncing off the ballroom ceiling, but she couldn't help herself, because it was true: this was a cheat. She half turned to the bird-thing on the balcony and bellowed her impotent fury.

"You cannot do this!"

But it could. It seemed to look at her, peering down that long, familiar beak, and then the staff in its hand moved fractionally, a tiny gesture that brought the swarm screaming down at them. Candace cried out, and Trina cut with her hands, sweeping the lights away, first one, then another, a desperate, frenzied series of movements somehow given skill, speed, and composure by the warrior angel within her. Trina cut and wheeled and parried, deflecting the murderous lights, sending them spinning away. But in each case, they regrouped and came again, varying their line of attack, feinting, speeding up and slowing down to throw her off. Still Trina fought, her face sweating, still she pulled her friend toward the ballroom steps and out beyond the velvet rope, conscious now that none of the others wearing the purple orchid had survived. Again the deadly lights amassed, spread, and dropped on them, and again Trina blocked and weaved.

She didn't see the one that got through. She just felt Candace stiffen in her arms. Trina pulled back to look at her friend, in time to see the shock in her face.

"I love you, Trina," she whispered.

For the merest fraction of a second, Trina saw her as she had been as an eleven year old, laughing uproariously from astride her painted wooden horse and brandishing a massive stick of cotton candy as if conducting the carousel music, and then Candace wasn't there anymore.

Trina howled, her embrace suddenly, horribly empty, a hole into which she might tumble herself. Tears flowed down her face, and she clamped her empty, weaponless hands to her temples, wailing her grief, her loss.

For a long moment, nothing happened, then Trina, emptied of emotion, turned, pointing up at the creature on the balcony.

"Why?" she shouted. A strange stillness had fallen on those in their white bubbles. The kids inside were staring, numb. The bird monster was silent too. "Well?" Trina demanded, her rage overmatching her fear. "Why are you doing this?"

The silence this time was longer still and then, unbearably, the monster started to whistle tunelessly as it had in the caves, a flat, empty sound, careless, flippant.

Trina's hands went to her ears to shut out the sound, but she felt the movement around her and revolved to see that the white protective bubbles that enclosed the survivors were melting away. As they did so, the orchids they were wearing wilted before their eyes, browning and shedding petals that evaporated before they hit the ground.

Trina wheeled around again. The monster's staff had

begun to glow again, and she knew what was coming. She turned back to the survivors.

"Run!" she commanded.

They had seen enough not to hesitate, but as they took to their heels, the bird-thing swept the staff up to his shoulder like he was sighting along the shaft of an arrow. A jet of lightning streamed from the head. Two students fell, but the staff's appalling energy did not just kill; it tore into the ballroom itself, shredding it. The explosion stripped away all that had made the chamber elegant and sophisticated, turning it back into a desolate, abandoned ruin so that there was no party and never had been. The paintings vanished, so did the chandelier, the punch bowl, and beneath the illusion was not the ragged Gothic monstrosity built by Treysville's eccentric Victorian magnates, but something lower and seedier, something of Formica and old food smells and a plastic chair with chrome legs, spinning as it fell.

Trina fled.

What was left of the party ran with her, a blind, screaming mass of bodies, thoughtless in their desire to get away. They pounded their way through the now-barren hall, stumbling in their haste, their desperation to be anywhere other than where they were. Overhead, the lightning flashed and exploded. Someone fell, though whether they had been hit or had merely tripped in the frenzy of retreat, Trina could not say. All she knew was that the crowd descending on the front door was too big, and the door that had seemed so broad and impressive when she had first arrived was now too narrow.

The bottleneck would be a killing ground.

She looked around wildly, even as she was borne forward by the stampede. To her right was an arched alcove flanked by pedestals, which may have once been topped by urns or statues. Trina fought her way through, shouting that they should follow her, they should take cover or, at very least, not all try to get out at once.

No one listened, and now the lightning was arcing through the fleeing students again and she was ducking and blundering out of the line of fire as best she could. The alcove was deeper than she had expected, but it was only when she reached the back that she saw a flight of stairs descending on each side. She chose one at random and vaulted down. At the bottom, she turned left and ran on down a featureless stone corridor, her driving footfalls almost drowned out by the pounding of her own heart.

She made two more turns, suddenly unsure which direction she was going or whether she was heading away from the core of the house or back into it. She was too busy listening to the blasts from the rooms above to notice when the stone underfoot became the featureless white tile of an antiquated hospital or some other bland, institutional building.

Strange.

She forced herself to keep going to the next corner, and the next, then stopped, lost and exhausted, bewildered by the change to her surroundings. In the next hallway, Trina saw an open doorway. Breathing hard, she stopped and looked inside.

It looked like a classroom, older than any at East Trey, all dark wooden desks, bookshelves, and an actual chalkboard. Sitting in front of the last, behind a massive desk of her own, was Miss Perkins, her unpleasant English teacher. She looked different from usual, her familiar pantsuit replaced by a tweed skirt and a demure blouse with a string of pearls around her neck, and she was wearing old-fashioned glasses that turned up at the corners like insect wings. She was grading a stack of deep blue, handwritten exercise books. Trina hesitated in the doorway, staring.

"Yes?" said Miss Perkins, barely looking up from her work.

"I'm sorry," said Trina, confused, "but you shouldn't be

here. There's a monster. It might come down here at any moment."

"A monster?" said the teacher with calm but withering scorn. "Yes, Miss Warren, that's the kind of nonsense I'd expect from you. Head in the clouds most of the time. I doubt you know what day it is."

"No, I mean it," Trina protested.

"So do I," said the teacher levelly. "Can you tell me what day it is?"

"What?"

"Would you like me to rephrase the question?"

"It's Monday," said Trina.

"No, you silly girl," said the teacher with deep contempt. "What holiday or festival is it?"

"Holiday?" said Trina blankly. "It's a school day. It's just a regular…"

"What nonsense!" snapped the teacher. "I swear, your work is consistently disappointing. This is particularly poor."

She scrawled with her pen in the exercise book she was marking and held it up for Trina to see. A bright red F had been scrawled across the page.

Trina peered at it, bewildered and outraged. How could she be sitting here working when above her something unspeakable was happening?

"That's not my work," she said.

"Plagiarism too!" said the teacher. "I might have known. Your father is going to be very disappointed in you, young lady. I don't see how you can possibly get into colleges with an honors code violation on your record, in addition to your generally shoddy grades. If you had even a modicum of athletic ability, I might see some way forward, but as it is… Well, at least your mother is not alive to see the full extent of your failure."

Trina swallowed. "That's a horrible thing to say," she said, staring fixedly because she knew that if she blinked her tears would spill out.

"I calls 'em as I sees 'em," the teacher replied with a nasty grin.

"You're a terrible person," said Trina flatly. "And a worse teacher. If you had any care for your students, you'd be up there, trying to help. But you're not. You're down here, *grading.*"

She said the last word with dismissive spite, but the teacher was unfazed.

"I can't do anything about whatever is happening upstairs," she said.

"You could try!" sputtered Trina. "You think you're so smart..."

"Oh, I am," said Miss Perkins. "Beyond smart. I am all knowing, or as near as makes no difference. But I can't help."

"Why not?" Trina shouted back.

"Oh, put it together, you silly girl!" snapped the teacher, giving her a hard, reptilian stare. "Because I'm already dead, obviously."

And at last Trina saw it, the blood, the wound she had somehow not noticed before. She put her hand to her mouth to hold in the scream. The teacher was lolling back in her chair, her head twisted around, motionless and utterly incapable of the conversation Trina had just heard.

Trina ran.

I*'ve gone mad*, she thought wildly as she turned corner after corner, stuck in the maze-like tunnels below the house. *That's the only explanation. I've seen more than I could handle and something inside me has broken.*

The angel within her, if there was such a thing, said nothing, but then Trina rounded a dingy corner and there were steps leading up to what may once have been a delivery drop, for coal or barrels. The wooden hatches at the top had rotted years ago, and the last few feet of the corridor were a mass of dead leaves and other stray detritus blown in by the elements. Mad or not, there might yet be a way out, and in her gut she felt sure that if she could get away from this place, everything would fall into place. If she could stop thinking about what had happened, stop seeing it in her head, then maybe,

maybe

she could move forward as a rational person. No more delusions, no more imaginary conversations with dead teachers. She caught herself at that, closing her eyes, sure that whatever else had happened, that bleak little grain of truth was undeniable.

Miss Perkins was dead.

"Where do you think you're going, Warren?"

Trina opened her eyes.

It was Kyle Martin. Of course, it was. And with him, grinning like hyenas, were Steve Parks and Colin Everett. They were standing between her and the hatch. They had not been there before.

"You're not real," she said, her voice low and weary. "You're probably dead."

"Do we look dead to you, loser?" snapped Steve.

"I don't think I know what death looks like anymore," she said, grief and exhaustion making her honest.

"You don't know anything," said Colin.

"Never did," added Kyle.

"You should go back," Steve concluded.

"Back?" said Trina flatly. "Back where?"

"Back to the dance," said Steve.

"Yeah," Kyle agreed. "There's nothing for you out this way."

Trina considered that, then took a step toward them.

"Don't you hear good, loser?" snapped Colin. "We said…"

"I don't care," Trina replied, and that too was honest. "You aren't real. You're just trying to stop me from fulfilling my destiny."

"You don't have a destiny," said Kyle.

"You're nothing," said Steve.

"If you did have a destiny, you would have stopped what happened at the dance," said Colin.

It was and was not the right thing to say. It felt all too true to Trina, a sword to her own heart, but it also made her furious.

"You're not real," she said again. "You are my doubts, my anxieties, my fears. And if you were right, and I really can't do anything to stop whatever is happening here, then you wouldn't have bothered coming. Now," she added, her voice steel hard, "get out of my way."

Trina walked through them. There was no fight as there had been when she saw them before, no flurry of tangled, flailing fists, no violence of any kind. She walked through them and they were gone. She paused before checking over her shoulder, taking in the empty corridor, then she breathed, her head sagging onto her breast, her eyes closed.

For a long moment, she just stood like that, trying to shut everything out, then she waded through the cobwebbed drifts of sticks and fallen leaves and paused below the hatch, listening. She could hear neither the screams of the fleeing students nor the explosions of the bird-thing's staff of power. She climbed an iron ladder set into the moldy brick wall and pushed her head up through the remains of the wooden doors. The darkness outside the Kitchener house was complete now and there was no one around. Slowly, suddenly wearier than she had ever been, she clambered free of the hatch and considered the grounds.

Without warning, it all came back to her, everything she had been running from, everything she had seen, everything she had been trying to avoid. Trina took a few quick steps and vomited into the grass beside an overgrown stone urn. Again and again she retched, till she felt hollowed out and lightheaded. Her throat burned and her eyes streamed, but that was nothing to the fire of shame and failure blazing within her. She had let them down, all of them, and Candace most of all. She sank into the tall grass and wept loud and long for her childhood friend who had wandered a little out of her social circle but was coming back, or would have if they had had just a little more time. Over and over, unbidden and unwanted, Trina saw Candace's open, guileless face whispering her love, seconds before the monster tore her apart. Trina would never hear her sing again, would never catch that wild rapture in her eyes as she lost herself in the music. There would be no carousel ride, no laughing, glorious snapshot of innocence and joy.

It was too painful to think about.

What the bird-thing had done to her was not just violence and disrespect. It was blasphemy, an abomination. He had reduced her to body, to muscle and bone, and other physical stuff: so much meat and chemical. *What* she was, not *who*. He had thrown her away like you might discard the bones and skin of a chicken leg, and he had hummed to himself as he did it. Why would anyone…?

Stop.

It was too much, and Trina felt the nausea rising again, wriggling up through her fury, her outrage, even though there was nothing left in her stomach to throw up. She pressed her forehead against the stone urn, leeching its cold into her skin as if she were dousing herself in water.

It helped. A little. Then she realized she was pressing so hard that she could feel the shrill whine of pain lancing through the cold. It was less than she deserved, and she pressed harder, gritting her teeth against the hurt in her forehead...

"*Stop.*"

She had told herself the same thing a moment earlier, but this time the word came from slightly outside herself, and she sat up abruptly staring around as if there might be someone standing behind her.

There wasn't, and Trina immediately knew who had spoken.

The angel, the warrior spirit that had bound itself to her and that she had all but forgotten in her failure. It had only given her three instructions so far: *Run, hide,* and, when those had proved insufficient, *fight.* Now it told her to stop, but she couldn't.

"I failed," she said aloud. "And not just because I didn't have a weapon. I ran away. I ran because I was afraid."

"*As you should be,*" whispered the angel within her. Its voice was calm as moonlight on a still pond, deep as the pond itself, and loaded with knowledge, with insight. "*Fear is good. You are still alive, and that means you can still fight.*"

"I can't," Trina said, admitting it at last. "I thought I could but... He's too strong, and I am...insufficient."

She had been about to say "weak," or "alone," but this seemed better, more exact. Trina thought that the precision of the term might stop the angel's obvious counterargument, but the spirit within her spoke again in the same serene voice as before.

"*I am with you,*" it said.

Trina shook her head.

"I can't," she replied to the night.

"*I will help,*" said the angel, still placid as night.

"I didn't ask for this," said Trina, suddenly defiant. "I didn't want it. I *don't* want it. I want to run away and hide. I want to weep for my friend. For all of them. I don't want to feel like it's my fault they are gone."

"It was not."

"It was! I'm impervious! I should have fought him, in there," she said, jerking her head toward the house, "or in the caves when I had the chance!"

"You couldn't."

"I could!"

"He would have killed you."

"So I can only be a hero when I know for sure that I'm safe? What use is that to anyone? I should have attacked him regardless of what happened to me," shouted Trina, crying again now but also angry. "But I didn't because I was just the same terrified loser I've always been."

"That's not true."

"It is! People died, and I couldn't stop it."

"Yes."

"That's all you've got? Yes? What use is that?"

"None, but it is true, nonetheless. You cannot save everyone, Trina. No one can."

"I couldn't save *anyone!*" she wailed. Her empty stomach had twisted itself into a hard knot of despair. She buried her tear-streaked face in her hands and sobbed raggedly.

"You weren't ready," said the angel. *"You will be."*

The voice was so even, so unrattled by Trina's anguish, that it stopped her. She crumpled where she sat and, for a long time, said nothing, though she shook her head sadly in answer to what the angel had said and to all that had gone before. She wouldn't be ready. Ever.

"You will," said the angel, knowing her thoughts.

Trina sat quite still, and when she finally spoke, the single syllable she uttered carried more than rhetorical defiance or weariness: it was colored by the merest shimmer of hope.

"How?" she said.

"*First,*" said the angel, "*you must be armed.*"

"I tried to get the swords off the wall in the house," said Trina miserably, "but they were too high, and I couldn't just *will* them to me."

"*They would not have helped,*" said the angel kindly.

"I thought…" Trina began, then faltered. "Percy said this place had a secret armory or something that I might be able to use."

"*In a sense he was right,*" said the angel. "*There is a weapon here for you and only you, an ancient blade of powerful enchantment. I can show you where it is, but it will take great strength to achieve it, and that must come from you alone.*"

Trina stared off into the black, shrouded mounds and spikes that were the trees of the untended estate and thought vaguely that talking to the angel was like talking on the phone when you couldn't see the face of the person who had called. She had always preferred FaceTime and other video calling apps for chatting with her friends because you could see their eyes, watch them laugh. It wasn't just that it was easier to read the silences. It was almost like you were together. Candace had used to love that…

Trina looked down at her hands. They were scratched and bruised, though she didn't know when that had happened. In the caves, maybe.

"This weapon," she began.

"*A sword.*"

"This sword then. Where is it?"

"*Come,*" said the angel. "*I will show you.*"

The voice did not come again, and for a while, Trina considered ignoring it and staying where she was. She thought of Candace who was dead, and Jasmine who might not be, and the thought filtered through her head that though she had failed, and though it was likely that she would fail again, she would not be able to live with herself if she did not try.

Sighing, she got up, and that itself was hard, a straining and wrenching that was more than the protests of her battered body. She hesitated and was about to demand of the angel which way she was supposed to go when she realized that she already knew. Slowly, Trina threaded her way down the weedy path to what had been a geometrically laid out formal garden, all raised beds, boxwood hedges, and yew trees once sculpted into interesting shapes, now wild, outlandish, and muffled with kudzu. The strange mixture of the meticulously laid out and its jungle-like evolution was oddly unsettling, like when a grackle had somehow flown in through her bedroom window and had not been able to figure out how to get out. It had gone mad, shrieking and flapping about, and though the bird was small and totally harmless, Trina had been petrified. It had just felt so wrong: the wild, animal thing among her books and photographs and stuffed toys. That was what the Kitchener grounds felt like, all that careful organizing human labor invaded and reclaimed by wildness. It made her uneasy.

Trina moved through a chaos of plantings, which might once have been a maze, and came to a vast openness, flashing blackly: a still, dark lake. She sighed again, this time smiling sadly because she remembered it from when she had come with her parents all those years ago. The lip of the pool was paved and regular, and though parts of it were cracked and weedy, it showed signs—unlike the rest of the estate—of having been maintained: there was a wooden jetty, which looked solid enough, and moored at the end was a small boat. The lake was broad, and it was too dark to see all the way across, but the implication was clear.

"The sword is on the other side?" said Trina, not liking the idea. "I have to cross the lake?"

"*Not all the way,*" said the angel.

This was offered as a compromise, but the prospect of sailing out into the middle where the water was probably deepest and stopping there rather than going all the way to land on the other side seemed somehow worse. Trina thought of the boat scene in *Harry Potter and the Half Blood Prince*, when Harry and Dumbledore had been seeking one of the horcruxes, and the water had been teeming with...

But that had been in a cave, she told herself, pushing the memory away with a shudder. *And besides, it was just a story.*

The boat was small but sleek, painted white inside and out but darker below the waterline. Trina climbed cautiously in, steadying herself on the jetty as the boat bobbed and shifted beneath her, and sat down facing the front, what she thought was called the prow. She checked the oars on their little pivots before unlashing the rope that kept the boat moored to the wooden pier. Trina knew nothing about boats and was generally afraid of them and the water they sailed on, but this felt as if it had been prepared specially for her. She knew that was crazy. Some local had obviously maintained the boat. Probably came here fishing for bass or catfish.

Trina took a breath and worked the oars. The boat drifted away from the dock, and she leaned instinctively into the oar stroke. In moments, they were moving smoothly, gliding in even surges with each stroke of the oars. There was something comforting in the easy rhythm she was able to establish without trying, and gradually her former despair peeled away as if they had left it on dry land. The angel within her said nothing as the boat carved its slow way out across the still water, but Trina felt sure she would know if she was heading in the wrong direction. From time to time she peered into the water as the oars cut the surface, but she saw only the silty swirl just below the surface. It was too dark to see how deep the water was, how tangled with weeds, and what might live amongst them. Normally that would have scared her, but she felt a sense of purpose, and not only because she suspected the angel was muting her fear of the water: Trina had seen far greater horrors than anything the lake might present.

Even so, after a few minutes rowing, Trina turned to look back the way they had come and couldn't help being a little unnerved at just how behind them the jetty was. From here it was almost invisible in the darkness, while the house was a mere shadow of an outline; there were no lights, no music, no vestige of the party venue. In fact, it seemed to have become once more the ruined Gothic castle she had first seen when she had entered the grounds. But as she gazed back, she saw a faint glow, not from the distant shore, but in the wake of the boat itself, a spangled phosphorescence that trailed behind them. It looked ghostly though it was, she told herself, probably some form of microalgae or bioluminescent plankton that the boat's passage had stirred to the surface. She had read about them in biology. It smelled too, not of the dank and weedy mud she had noted before, the flat wetness of still ponds and the creatures that lived in them, but something strangely manmade and familiar.

Chlorine?

That couldn't be right, she thought, but that was what it smelled like—a sharp, synthetic tang that reminded her of swim meets and summer trips to the Y with her dad and...

"*There*," said the angel abruptly.

Trina turned forward again, focusing and gazing about her, and saw that the luminescence of the water wasn't just behind them. It was everywhere, and it was concentrated directly ahead of the boat where the strange glow condensed and intensified as if there were a pool of light within the lake. The water there was a bright aquamarine, swirling with spangles as if lit by some powerful lamp from below, bright enough to cast shadows in the little boat and wash Trina's skin and clothes in a pearly glow. She leaned forward and peered down over the prow and had the strange but powerful feeling that the light came not from the lakebed itself, but from somewhere else entirely so that the spot felt like a vortex or...

A portal.

Yes. The light came from somewhere else entirely, and as the boat glided noiselessly toward it, the water below swirled and foamed as the bright effervescence from below the surface stirred into flickering brilliance.

Something was coming up.

It rose in a boiling, silvery haze that churned the waters of the lake and broke the surface like a fountain of light.

Within that unearthly pillar of white, blazing energy was a long, bright blade pointing into the sky as if driving back the darkness. It came all the way out, three feet of fine steel burnished on both edges and coming to a needle-sharp point. As it emerged from the water, the light below the surface dwindled to nothing, but the brilliance in the air above increased tenfold and Trina shielded her eyes. The sword's cross guard was silver or platinum, but it was ornamented with a blue-white stone mounted just above the handle, a stone that shone so brightly that Trina found she could not look directly at it. Stranger still, its handle was gripped by a strong female hand.

The sword rose up, dripping, elegant, and graceful as the arm that bore it, and Trina could just make out a woman in the undulating shadows beneath the surface, white, gauzy clothes and long hair both stirred by the tumult in the water. The figure's eyes and mouth were closed as if she were asleep, but she looked strangely familiar. Before Trina could study the face, however, the angel's voice appeared in Trina's head, and the message was clear.

"Take it," she said. *"This is for you."*

Trina reached out her hand and clasped the handle. Immediately the other hand released it to her and sank beneath the surface of the lake. Trina looked down, as compelled by the woman who had given it to her as the gift itself, but the light beneath them had already faded significantly, and in seconds, it had dwindled to nothing.

Even the glow coming from the sword itself was shrinking steadily, the crystal in its hilt dimming till it might have merely been diamond or glass, a pretty thing cut to reflect the light outside itself. Instinctively Trina knew that this was a kind of sleepy disguise, that the power within the stone had not gone completely. It would come when she called it.

She was sure of that.

Because the sword was hers. She held it out in front of her, as if learning its characteristics. It was light, and it balanced perfectly in her hand as if made for her and her alone, though—like the miniature on the necklace—it resembled the Destiny Sword. When she considered it closely, she saw that the gem in its hilt hadn't dulled completely; there was still a spark of light within it. It throbbed faintly, as if it were alive. Trina stood up, legs splayed to keep the boat balanced, and raised the sword over head straight up, a Jedi knight, a hero of Camelot. The knives she had wielded before had felt like an extension of her arm. This felt similarly, except that it immediately became hard to imagine not having it. It was as if something she had been too young for before, but which was always going to come, had finally arrived. Her life to date became prehistory, and she was new born, the way she was meant to be. Trina the high school student was gone. Trina the warrior angel leapt into being like Athena springing fully armed from the head of Zeus, new but also, finally, complete.

She laid the sword in the boat beside her and addressed herself to the oars again, but the blade smoldered in her mind as if tethered to her consciousness. It pulsed with Trina's own life blood. It breathed with her. It shrilled to her peril.

Trina's senses flared with alarm.

Because as the boat turned back toward the distant jetty, there was a new disturbance in the water, and this brought with it no holy glow, no promise of salvation. It began merely as a rippling of the dark water, which swelled, thick and oily, buffeting the boat so that it rocked violently.

"What's happening?" said Trina, but the angel was silent, so silent, in fact, that it was as if the spirit had never been there at all. Then she remembered what the angel had said about their being a trial involved in taking the sword, one that would test her strength and hers alone.

Whatever was coming, Trina would have to face it without guidance.

That is fine, she thought, laying her hand to the hilt of the sword, just below the blue-white stone. She was ready. The sword thrilled to her touch, and its power coursed through her.

The black water began to boil like tar, but Trina stood up, the sword's long haft gripped in both hands before her, daring the world to throw whatever it had at her, but perfectly composed and at peace. She was Beowulf, swimming out to sea and cutting at the monsters that attacked him with his long sword. She was mistress of the waters.

Impervious...

The lake surface in front of her belched suddenly, and objects surfaced, some pale, some dark. At first she thought they were statues, or parts of statues, though she didn't understand why statues would float or why they would be wearing clothes.

And then she recognized the faces from the dance hall, and her calm and self-possession buckled. The thick and viscous pitch of the lake threatened to invade her mind, to drown it. It was too appalling. For a moment the night swam, and she seized the side of the boat with her free hand to stop herself from falling, closing her eyes against the terrible apparitions. She was breathless, feeling the urge to weep paralyzing her again, but then she seized on something hotter that the shock had muffled. It was more than anger. It was fury.

She braced herself and opened her eyes, looked deliberately at the bodies, not pushing the horror away but refusing to quail in the face of it. In that instant she knew that if the bird-monster had sent them to sap her courage, to break her will, it had failed. The scale of his monstrosity only gave her fire.

And he would burn for it.

The thought seemed to spread beyond her and, as if the lake itself sensed her resolve, the bubbling subsided, and the bodies began to sink once more, the water closing over them like oil. But it was not over. Trina was allowed only a second to savor her small victory before the boat jarred and, with an awful, splitting sound like tearing fabric, two great spines stabbed up through the keel.

It was chaos. The little vessel lifted bodily into the air as if pivoting on its stern, turning slightly as the weight of the thing that had stabbed through from below completed its surging lunge and fell back below the surface. Trina was flung backward, flailing as she tried to reach the oar locks. She caught hold, but was badly off balance and crumpled into an uneven squat at the back of the crippled boat. The spines that had pierced the hull were longer than she was tall, pale and pointed, spiraled like unicorn horns, though they were only a few inches apart and clearly came from the same beast. The boat's planked bottom was cleanly punctured, and the weight of the creature splashing back into the lake wrenched the boards apart. There was a great, wrathful floundering in the black water, and the hole in the boat through which the water was erupting like a geyser tore lengthwise. The timber frame at the prow buckled and the boat split in half.

Trina, fumbling to keep hold of the sword, rocked to one side, then the other, and then she was in the water with the horned beast, blind and sputtering. The boat was simply gone.

Trina reached down with her feet in the hope that the lake was shallow enough to stand in, but she felt only insubstantial things below her, though whether they were weed, fish, or something considerably worse, she could not say. The water closed over her face, and she had to work her legs hard to regain the surface. Gulping the night air, she trod water furiously. There was no sign of the bodies, and the water was calm again, if only for a moment, so that she was able to rub her eyes clear and steel herself for whatever would happen next.

At least she still had the sword. It was gripped tight in her right hand like a lifeline. It was too much to hope that the thing that had speared her boat and split it into kindling would not come back. The attack had been deliberate, targeted.

Trina turned in place, scanning for signs of her assailant and kicking steadily as she adjusted to her natural buoyancy, the sword raised just above the surface. It didn't feel heavy enough to weigh her down, but she couldn't swing it in any meaningful way. The lake was still, so that only the fragments of wreckage hinted at what had just occurred. Of the creature responsible, there was no sign at all.

Trina kicked steadily, scanning vigilantly, breathing through her nose as the water lapped at her lips, turning left and right, rotating in place...

There!

She happened to be looking back toward the dock when she saw something long and slick and gray arch its back above the surface like a whale taking a breath, then diving. It was moving easily but not fast, cruising in a broad arc that swept around toward the shore on her right. She watched the ripples as it vanished below the surface. For a while it was gone, but then she saw it again, the merest disturbance in the water as it breached then returned to the same shallow curve; it was just below the surface, and it was circling her.

Trina turned with it, like the center of the wheel of which the horned beast was the rim. It was getting faster, as if winding itself up for an attack. She had seen little of it when it had rammed through the boat, but it had looked like the two parallel horns stuck directly out from its face. Though they were sharp at the tip, they were rounded along their lengths like rods. They were tools for stabbing, not cutting.

So it will try to spear me, she thought, scanning the lake, taking in once more the strangely chemical smell she had noticed before.

Chlorine...

Almost immediately she felt a pulse of power through the water. The great beast that had been cruising easily had broken from its circular arc, turned inward, and beaten its tail hard to give it thrust. It was coming for her, and it was coming fast. She turned into its attack, spotting its wake, mind teeming even as she trod water. She couldn't see it, but she sensed it closing like a torpedo, precise and unflinching.

Steeling herself for the impact, Trina placed her left hand

on the sword handle and lowered it into the water as far as her belly. Immediately the stone in its hilt began to glow steadily brighter, and the water around her lit up softly for several yards in all directions. She held the sword out in front of her with the blade vertical, its turned edge forward. It felt more like a talisman than a weapon. If she mistimed her movement, the beast would skewer her where she was.

The next throb of the creature's tail was so powerful that it almost washed her onto her back, but she rode out the swell and, as the wave reached her, caught the merest flash of the pale horn tips in the glow of her sword just below the surface. They were lancing directly for her gut. She adjusted the sword an inch or two, no more, waited as the deadly points slid past her blade, then, as the gem in the hilt pulsed with new brilliance, she pushed the sword hard to the right. It caught the horns precisely, the movement small but exact, doing just enough to clear the horns so that they slid by her ribcage.

The beast's head, hard as the head of a rubber mallet, met her in the midriff. She gasped, wincing slightly to the left to let it go by, but released the sword with her left hand. Then as it shot past, she rolled back into the creature, throwing her free hand over its back, and scrambling for purchase on its slick, leathery hide. There was nothing to hold, but she clamped herself to it like a lamprey, squeezing for dear life as she reversed her grip on the sword with her right hand. The creature bellowed, blasting foul-smelling air, water, and mucus from its blow hole, and then dived. Trina gulped oxygen before being dragged down, and together they shot toward the lake bottom, twisting and turning as the beast fought to throw her off.

Desperately, certain that she could not afford to let it turn those horns on her, Trina clung on. She knew that she could not stay under anything like as long as it could, but she had no choice. It rolled along its length till it was upside down, driving her back and shoulders into the rock and sandbars of the lakebed, trying to scrape her off like old skin. Trina was gashed and buffeted, but she held on still, her eyes open and stinging,

chlorine sting,

trying to guide the sword tip into place. The blade was not designed for close fighting like this, however. It was too long. To use it, she would have to let the monster go.

And she was almost out of air. She could feel her stomach clenching, her throat beginning to spasm as if she were going to throw up. The stone in her sword handle glowed like a white-hot coal in the dark water.

It was now, or never.

She released the beast, felt it slide free of her and then, as it tried to turn back on itself, to impale her with its horns, she summoned all the strength she still had and swept the sword back across its underside. The sword moved slowly in the water, but she felt its edge bite and draw. Blood blossomed like thick, swirling smoke in the water, and then the beast was writhing and sputtering in its rage and pain. It was a terrible wound, she knew, perhaps even a fatal one, but it would not kill the monster quickly. Even so, she was amazed that it did not flee, turning instead to face her. As it did so, one of its horns slapped her lengthways in the shoulder, knocking her back.

She gasped and her lungs flooded.

She fought for the surface, kicking furiously, spitting her mouth empty the instant she felt the air on her face. She retched, momentarily forgetting the creature she had been battling in her desperate need to breathe. Suddenly she just had to get out of the water. She turned, scanning the shore for the closest point, never thinking that the malice of the injured beast would bring it back. Wheezing, amazed to be alive, Trina set out for a rocky outcrop surrounded by reeds only a few dozen yards away with a ragged and uneven crawl.

This time Trina sensed nothing as the crippled beast lumbered back around and knifed its way through the water toward her. She was too tired, too relieved, too unprepared for the speed and ferocity of its attack. When she realized what was happening, it was too late. Her parry was slow, clumsy, and ineffectual. One of the creature's horns caught her under her left arm and ran her through.

The pain was unspeakable, a shaft of white-hot agony which tore clean through her arm. For one awful second, Trina felt her body lifted right out of the water by the thrust, saw with horror how the great spike came out the other side. She threw back her head and howled, thinking nothing, feeling nothing. She looked down into the creature's glassy black eyes. She saw it open its vast mouth, the scabrous lips folding back on themselves as if trying to swallow her whole.

With a twitch of her right hand, the sword tip slid into the creature's hungry, gleeful maw, and with what she knew would be the last act she could muster before blacking out, she thrust it home.

Again, the creature lashed and flailed as the sword skewered it, reawakening the torture of her shoulder, and then it was still and sliding away under its own weight, dragging its horn out of her as it sank. Trina rolled onto her back, gasping, her right hand clamping against the hole in her shoulder.

It was only then that she realized the awful truth. In the last breath of the fight, when the agony had taken her completely, she had dropped the sword. It had been plucked from her hand by the weight of her victim. It was gone now. Lost forever. Sobbing quietly, Trina floated, staring up at the night sky, and had just enough time to think once more that she had failed, before the pain and blood loss overwhelmed her at last, and she lost consciousness.

Trina drifted, her eyes closed. She felt strong, supple hands on her wound and heard whispered words in a language she could not understand. A spell or incantation perhaps, a prayer. That was what they felt like: a request or a hope made in words. She was still floating, could feel the dark water all about her, and when she got her eyelids to flutter apart, she saw nothing at first, just water and weed and the black hole in her shoulder around which the water ran red. But then she saw the woman in the water, the same sleeping face and floating hair as she had seen when she got the sword.

The sword!

She fought to speak, to tell the lake-woman that she had lost that most precious of gifts, but a voice came, whispering, soothing, though she still did not know the words or what they meant, and Trina slid once more into unconsciousness.

13

Trina woke wet and cold. She was on her back, lying on pebbles. Where she had taken the boat, the shore had been crafted stone blocks. She opened her eyes wearily and turned her head, trying to process where she was. The stony beach was almost a cove surrounded by trees.

The far side of the lake, then. A quarter mile or more from the Kitchener house.

For a while, she lay where she was, content to breathe, to be alive. Then, as the memories of dreadful things she had managed to forget in her slumber swept back over her, she groaned, one hand sliding to the hole in her shoulder. She found it dressed with bandages of some strange, fine weave. She considered this, baffled, but conscious that the wound, which should have been caked with blood, which might—indeed—have been the end of her, was merely tender. She put a little cautious pressure on it, testing the edges of the injury through the bandage, finding it smaller, tighter than the wide and ragged hole it should have been. When she felt ready, she attempted sitting up and found that she could.

Tentatively she moved the arm. It ached with stiffness, but there was none of the bright, shrieking pain she had expected.

Strange. Good, of course, but strange.

That wasn't all. Shifting position had revealed another blessed surprise: the sword, bright and unmarked from her battle in the water, lay on the shingle beside her.

Trina's heart leapt.

She rose cautiously, unsure her legs would hold her, but she felt…okay. Soaked to her skin and cold, but yes, okay. Good, even. Her previous scrapes and bruises seemed to have gone, and when she put a little weight on her twisted ankle testingly, there was no answering twinge. Amazed, she found that she felt almost whole, and while she would like to put down her miraculous recovery to some hidden reserve of strength or a gift from the warrior angel, the dressing and the presence of the sword told her that the ethereal woman in the lake had saved her. Her touch had been tender, nurturing, but also familiar. This was no dryad or water spirit.

"Mom?" she said.

No sound came in reply, and though that was, in its way, heartbreaking, it made her stop and think. She knew it made no sense. She knew her mother was dead, struck down not by magic or monsters but by a cancer that had been infuriatingly prosaic and ordinary, something Trina would not have been able to fight even now with her sword and her angel gifts. Her mother could not be here.

And yet. Whatever had been in those dark waters had saved her, and she would not give up the possibility that somehow, however obliquely, that presence had known her, loved her, laughed with her at a carousel ride not far from this very spot.

"Thank you," she said, turning to face the water and laying one hand on her heart.

There was no reply, but she didn't need one. Despite her sense of escape, however, Trina was uncomfortable so close to the lake and still in view of the castle-mansion where the dance massacre had taken place, and she was pleased to turn her back on both. A narrow path led up from the beach, and though she could not see where it led for the dark and heavy trees that crowded it, it seemed as good a way to go as any.

Right?

She stood there, dripping, considering the path, repeating the rationale to herself to prompt a reply. Better this way than returning to the house.

Yes?

She listened for the warrior angel, but the spirit had said nothing since Trina had first found the sword. She still felt the acuteness of her senses, the strength and elegance of her own movements, and she knew that those were gifts from the angel, but she didn't know what she was supposed to do next: some guidance would be useful. She framed the idea deliberately in her head, laying out the desire for help and waiting for a response from the spirit.

Nothing happened and, after a moment of just standing there as if paralyzed, the silent emptiness of her own thoughts began to feel oppressive, and Trina started walking up the path, squeezing the lake water from her hair.

She had assumed the track would lead directly up through the woods to the estate's perimeter wall, but it cut back on itself several times, the ground rising constantly. The path itself was roughly compacted field stone, and judging by the tree limbs she had to duck or clamber over, it hadn't been in regular use for decades. Between the larger trees were scraggy cedars and sprawling rhododendrons, their leaves almost as large and thick as magnolias, their limbs so long and heavy that they touched the ground like the elbows of old men unable to sustain their own weight.

She pressed on, and was beginning to think she was going nowhere helpful when she saw something sparkle in the moonlight just off the path. She stooped to it and picked it up; it was a tiny cylindrical amulet, brass, and marked with a familiar insignia: the head of a bird. It loomed a little like Thoth, the ibis-headed Egyptian god, though she couldn't remember what he was god of.

Death? No, that was Anubis.

She ran her fingers over the amulet, feeling its coldness, the hollow top just above the shoulder, and something of her previous outrage returned, as did a flash of triumph: she was on his trail. She pocketed the amulet and felt it chink against something else. Her fingers explored and closed around a smooth, oval object. She drew it out.

It was the blue plastic egg with a seam around the middle that the boy in glasses had given her.

She considered it, thinking back to the time before the nightmare in the ballroom, and went to open it, but even as she gripped the two halves ready to pull them apart, she remembered what the boy had said.

"Don't open it. Not till the very end."

Which end? she wondered vaguely. The dance was long over, but she didn't think he had meant that, and she clearly had more yet to do. Frowning, she slipped the unopened egg back into her pocket. From somewhere overhead, she heard a low rumble.

Thunder, she thought, except that it didn't stop. It rolled on and on, building steadily, and as she looked up through the oaks and sweetgums, she saw that the night sky was swirling with a strange green energy. Trina made a few quick strides up the path to where the trees thinned, and she was able to get a better look. The storm, if that was what it was, flickered and pulsed with bright spots that were almost white in their intensity, but it was no ordinary lightning that was building there. The cloud was thickening and concentrating with unnatural speed, and the light within gave a peculiar lime cast to the world below like the unnerving greenish stillness that came sometimes when you were under a tornado watch. She stood there, gazing up apprehensively, and then the sky rippled as if it were tearing open. There was a crescendo in the dragging roar, which brought her hands to her ears, and the brilliance within the cloud flared. It stabbed down in a ragged jet, a column of electricity that plunged into the earth like a hammer stroke.

Trina couldn't see where it landed, but she heard the blast of the explosion, saw the yellow-green flash at the impact point, and she felt the ground shake. This was the work of the enemy. There was no question about that.

She needed to get under cover, and fast.

She had only gone a few yards, however, when the thunder spiked again. She caught the same undulation in the heavens and glanced up as a second column of light smashed to the ground and lit the night.

Closer, she thought. *Definitely.*

It was too much to hope that that was coincidence. Someone, or something, was guiding whatever was happening up there, and at the very least they knew roughly where she was.

Trina picked up the pace. There was a lull in the thunderous rumbling, but only for a few seconds. Then it was building again, and the light overhead was moving as if it were searching.

For you, she thought to herself. *For you, or for the sword or the necklace. It doesn't matter which.*

The next strike was even brighter, its sickly light flashing off the trees around her and throwing long, menacing shadows, but the sound of its impact was different. It sizzled and crackled with electricity, and in place of an explosion there was a dull hiss that built into a crash of water.

The lake.

Which was only a few hundred yards behind her. Trina felt the hairs on her arms and the back of her neck stand up as the static wave reached her, but she kept moving, her eyes raking the woods for cover. She rounded a bend in the track, vaulting a rotten tree trunk covered in strange fungi and poisonous-looking mushrooms, and then she felt it again, the build before the strike. It was close now, almost directly overhead, and she had the presence of mind to hurl herself to the ground.

The explosion uprooted trees and tore up clods of earth and undergrowth, which flew in all directions. It blasted a clearing whose edge was no more than twenty yards from where she lay. For a moment, the world had gone white, and then it was dark and smoking, the night thick with dust and smoke and the ozone scent of the charged air. There were little fires everywhere, flickering and sparking. Trina rolled, desperate now, feeling the heat all around her, knowing that she could not survive a direct hit, sword or no sword. She risked a look up and around. By the light of one of the flames to her right, she saw a narrow gully in the forest floor, its edges curiously sharp and geometrical.

Stone blocks.

Her eyes traveled up what was surely a drainage channel that flowed down the hill to the lake, and she saw that some ten yards farther up, there was what looked like a large black letter box: an opening, where the drain vanished under the ground. It would be tight, perhaps too tight, but if she could get inside…

She scrambled toward it, her left hand pushing on the earth as she loped raggedly toward the culvert, hoping beyond hope that it would be wide and deep enough to shelter her from the malevolent storm that seemed to be pursuing her.

It was. Just. She dived in, headfirst, catching her hip on the sharp, angled stones at the mouth of the drain, then she was fighting her way forward on her hands and knees, wriggling inside as another strike from above lit the forest and filled the drainage channel with deafening echoes.

The roof of the channel pressed into her shoulders as she pushed forward, and the bottom was wet with foul smelling silt, but she was definitely safer here than outside. She slid the sword awkwardly into her belt—she could not brandish it in here, whatever she might encounter—and crawled on. As Trina moved she became aware that the almost complete darkness of the culvert had softened considerably so that she could see her way through the stone channel, the sides of which were lit by a faint blue-white radiance: it was the stone in her sword hilt. It had awoken at her unconscious need, and the fact of that cheered her a little.

On she crawled. It was close in the passage, but she was still damp from the lake and had started to shiver. At one point she thought she had gone as far as she could, but the mass in front of her turned out to be mostly moss and cobweb—a nest of some sort, she suspected—but she was able to shove her way through, spitting debris, deliberately not speculating at what might have been living down here. Her knees groaned and her palms stung from the grit and animal bones she was surely moving through, but the passage was straight and secure. From time to time, she felt the ground tremble and heard the bass piano crash of another impact on the ground above, but the drainage duct had taken her deeper into the very stone of the hill.

Once the stone beneath her buckled and popped, as if the whole was not stone at all, but sheet metal, hollow underneath, and she was suddenly, unaccountably afraid that someone would hear her there. Trina kept still till the feeling passed, smelling the damp of her hair and clothes, baffled once more by the curious odor of chlorine, then went back to her meticulous crawl on all fours.

The culvert ended abruptly in a cast iron grate.

She had seen it from several yards back, but had kept going anyway, hoping against hope that it would prove less secure than it looked, but she was badly disappointed. The grate was solid metal an inch thick, cast into a crisscross of solid beams designed to filter out the larger debris from the water as it drained. It was pitted and brownish with rust, which, with her heightened senses, smelled like blood, but it was sturdy nonetheless. Trina pushed at it with all the strength she could summon, but it did not move even an iota. She tried again without success. The grate was both heavy and, it seemed, locked in place. It occurred to her that it might not open at all, that it had been mortared in place when the drain had been built. A foot beyond the grate, she could smell the forest air, but she couldn't reach it.

Despairing, thinking that she was going to have to go all the way back and risk the terrible storm after all, she collapsed, face down, head turned to the side, sucking in the fetid air. She wondered if she turned around and kicked at the grate with her feet that that might shift it, but the culvert was too tight even to make the attempt. She tried reaching through the grate in case there was a release lever on the other side but could only get her hand through as far as her elbow. It wasn't enough.

She collapsed again, fighting down a sob, then took another long, steadying breath. Strength alone would not get it done, and she refused to give up without trying every other possibility. She slid the sword out of her belt and moved its luminous handle close to the grate so she could see it better. Perhaps if she slid the blade through and tried to use it as a lever?

And break the sword in the process? No.

Unable to make out anything that helped, she sheathed the sword again and grasped the grate in both hands once more. She pushed with all the force she had but it did not budge, both sides sitting tightly in the heavy iron grooves of the frame, so that she collapsed onto her chest again, panting. She felt the special exhaustion of defeat swelling within her.

Grooves, she thought idly.

Maybe the grate wasn't designed to be pushed or pulled open and maybe, she thought, hope lighting within her like the smallest candle, it wasn't locked as she had assumed. After all, who would bother locking a drain? Maybe it was supposed to be pulled up from above…

Trina rolled onto her back and scooched up to the grate so that the top of her head pressed against the metal. Then she reached back with both hands and gripped one of the horizontal bars of the grate as if she were lifting weights in a gym. She braced herself with her knees against the stone roof of the duct and pushed not forward, but up.

At first nothing happened, but then she felt the faintest shifting of the metalwork. She took a break, breathing hard, then tried again, and this time, with a shower of dirt and grit that fell into her eyes and mouth, the grate slid upward. It was only a couple of inches, but it was enough for her to find the strength to continue. She shuffled a little further for leverage and tried again. It was a little easier this time, and as soon as she felt the bottom of the grate clear her head, she wriggled all the way under it, twisting her face to the side as she did so, her teeth gritted. If her strength failed her now, it would pin her, maybe even crack her skull open.

Don't think that. Push.

She pressed again, harder than ever, growling like the thunder outside, building to a shout as the grate slid up and, with a soft, metallic thunk, latched in place.

Trina pulled her way under it in a frenzied rush, grasping

the mouth of the drain and hauling herself out and onto the woodland floor. She was cold and filthy, her hair and clothes smeared with foulness and stuck with leaf litter and God knew what else, but she was out. In her relief, it took her several seconds to realize that the terrible storm had stopped. She lay where she was, wiping the muck from her face, sucking in the forest air. Then she got up, drew her sword, and surveyed her situation. The woods were denser here, but that only showed the path more clearly. Without another thought, she set out along it, moving up and away from the lake. Whatever she might yet achieve, she wouldn't do it here, and she was running out of time. She didn't know why she thought that, or what was going to happen next, and the angel—if it was still there—said nothing either way, but she was certain she had to move on and quickly. Somewhere, somehow, she may yet do a little good, and that might redress some of her failure, her guilt. She pressed on.

A dozen yards up the trail, the path stepped up over a pair of boulders where part of the track had been washed away. In the remaining clay was a fresh shoe print. It looked curiously ordinary, a heel and toe impression marked by the tread marks of a mass-produced boot or sneaker. She wasn't sure what this could have to do with the bird-headed monster, but she thought of the amulet she had found earlier and knew they were connected. That unsettled her a little, though what she had expected the bird-thing to wear on its feet, she couldn't say. Still, she proceeded with caution, extending the tip of the sword out in front of her like a torch as she completed the climb.

The woods seemed a little less random here, and as she moved forward, the path became a tunnel, cutting through a dense thicket of holly trees, the kind with glossy oval leaves and a single spine on the end. Where it had been winding and indirect before, the track was suddenly straight and made of bricks packed into the ground. There was no trace of weeds or underbrush and the holly canopy was complete and vaguely surreal like something out of *Alice in Wonderland* or the *Chronicles of Narnia*. Trina kept the sword out in front of her and moved forward until she was sure she could see a light ahead.

It was soft and bluish: an old-fashioned gas lamp in a wrought-iron hanger. She moved a few paces farther along the holly tunnel and saw that it was mounted on a stone structure directly ahead. Beside the lamp was a weather-beaten door, but it wasn't until she emerged from the passage entirely that she could see what she was looking at.

It was a tower, round and tall, with a rampant lion sten-ciled on the side in faded yellow paint. She was too close to see the top of the building and could not guess what purpose it had served. A fanciful watch tower designed to match the faux castle, perhaps, a kind of Victorian folly? An amateur astronomer's observatory? Or maybe it had some more prac-tical function tied to the nearby lake, a pumping station perhaps. Anchored in the mortar was a precarious looking rusted pipe, with alternating rungs on each side, serving as a crude ladder up to the top.

Glinting in the gas lamp was another of the little brass amulets. It lay in the grass by the door, and Trina knew that she had to go inside. She thought of Sir Gawain approaching the ruined chapel to face the Green Knight, listening to the giant sharpening his huge axe...

She put her hand on the door's latch, squeezed it, and felt it open.

14

The door stuck on the threshold but opened wide under a little pressure from her shoulder. It was dim inside, but not dark. A soft light came from a bare, brownish bulb set above the lintel. The cable that supplied the light with power had been crudely stapled to the bare stone sometime after the original construction, but judging by the nature of the wire, which was cloth wrapped rather than plastic sheathed, not much after. Trina looked around. She was in the base of the tower, and the little chamber was dominated by a wooden staircase that spiraled up toward the top. It too looked old and worn, but sturdy enough, though ascending the cramped staircase before she knew what was at the top felt risky. At ground level, on the other side of the chamber, was an open doorway, which led into what appeared to be a hallway with other rooms leading off it. She decided to explore them first.

The hallway was spare but clearly domestic with a worn rug on its wooden floor. On one side was a room whose door was ajar and, nudging it wider, Trina saw a brass bed, old fashioned and basic, but apparently made up for use. There was a towel on a hook by the door, and she grabbed it, rubbing her hair and arms if only to stop the strangely chemical lake water from running into her eyes. Had there been spare clothes, she might have considered changing; the cold had seeped into her, wrinkling her skin and making her tremble.

Farther along the hall was a sitting room with a fireplace, and beyond that, a small and tidy kitchen with an enameled gas range and a deep, square sink with large, utilitarian taps of tarnished brass. Taken together it seemed clear that she was in a living space, basic and at least a hundred years old, but functional and somehow familiar.

So what function did the tower serve? Whoever had lived here had surely been employed in some way connected to it. She thought vaguely of windmills, but there was no trace of a mechanism to transfer power or motion from the top to the bottom, nor was there room for any. She drifted into the little lounge with the fireplace and settled into an ancient leather wingchair, feeling the weight of all she had done over the previous hours, physical and emotional. She knew she couldn't stay there long but, just for a moment, for a couple of minutes or less, she needed to just stop. As soon as she sat down, she felt all the punishment that had been visited upon her body, all the strain on her mind and heart, flare and then, almost immediately, begin to subside.

From the wingchair she considered the mystery of the place, uncomfortably aware that all the rooms were too small for her to wield the sword with any kind of efficiency. It was as she was considering the size of the rooms that she realized why they felt so familiar. She had visited a similar little cluster with her father on their first trip to Charleston after her mother had died, and they too had been built to serve a round tower.

It was a lighthouse. The instant the possibility occurred to her, it was obvious.

Why there was a lighthouse up here in the hills of North Carolina she had no idea. Perhaps it was another kind of folly built on a whim to go with the lake, though maybe it had once had a more serious purpose, now long forgotten.

And today? The monster or its agents had been on the path outside, and that meant they might still be here, up there in the tower. What dreadful purpose might they put the beacon to now?

"I hoped you'd come."

Trina got to her feet and stared back into the hall.

"Percy!" she exclaimed. "I thought... I couldn't find you after the... After the ballroom. You're okay!"

She felt the urge to run to him and throw her arms around his neck, but she held back. There had been too much grief and horror for that. In spite of her relief at seeing him, celebration of any kind felt wrong.

"Never better," he said with a wan smile. His face looked waxy, and the stain on his shirt where it covered the wound in his belly was dark and slick once more. "You have the sword," he said, eyeing it.

"Yes. It was in the lake. I was given it by the spirit in the waters, the woman."

"I thought that might happen," he said, smiling bleakly. "And you thought you weren't worthy."

Trina looked down, blushing, but she couldn't let the compliment pass. She didn't deserve it.

"I wasn't," she said. "I didn't get the sword till...after. If I'd had it at the dance, maybe..."

But she couldn't finish the sentence, and when he looked down awkwardly, she swallowed, blinked, and redirected.

"What are you doing here?" she asked.

"I can use the reflectors in the old lighthouse to

disrupt the barrier around the town," he said, walking over to a writing desk, pulling open a drawer and rummaging through it. "There's an old stone circle on the other side of the trees over there. I can use that to amplify the beam if I can get the light to shine right into it."

"The light?"

"I can generate a signal using power from the main lighthouse beacon," he said, as if it were obvious. "Tap into the power of the circle, and it will transmute the beacon and short circuit the screen that surrounds the town."

"That'll work?" asked Trina uncertainly. It all sounded so strange, like something out of *Star Trek* or *Doctor Who*. After all she had been through, she felt suddenly irrelevant and stood there shifting from foot to foot, self conscious about the way her wet clothes clung to her. She tried to smooth them out.

Percy tried another drawer and came up with what looked like an old-fashioned glass fuse, the kind with metal caps and a thin wire running through the center.

"Looks like," he said, brandishing the fuse with a grin. "Just give me a minute and I'll show you."

He continued sifting through the contents of the drawer, humming to himself.

No. Not humming.

Whistling through his teeth. A tuneless, casual sound she had heard before.

Trina stiffened, her mind blank, the world passing by in slow motion.

No. It can't be.

But the tuneless whistle went on just long enough for her to be sure. She didn't say anything, didn't demand to know what was going on, and she certainly didn't attack him. Not based on a whistle. That would be crazy. But she heard it, and it rooted her to the spot. Her mouth dry, she stared at him.

Whether it was the quality of her silence, or a sense of her eyes on him, Percy caught himself. The whistling stopped, and he became suddenly still. Then he smiled. It was a mirthless, reptilian look, smug and condescending.

It transformed him.

Trina felt tears hot in her eyes. It wasn't like puzzle pieces falling into place; it wasn't like everything now made sense. Quite the contrary. She knew now, but there had been no clues that explained this, and the shock of his abrupt switch from friend to enemy had her frozen with a dismay so profound that it achieved what the imaginary bullies outside the cave had so failed to. Confronted by just how little she had understood, let alone achieved, Trina gave up. Just for a moment, perhaps, but definitively and finally, because this was too much to bear. She remembered the way he had ushered her from the chapel before the monster arrived and —worse—the way he had vanished from the ballroom immediately before the bird-headed thing had appeared on the balcony with its staff of power. She had never seen him and the monster in the same place at the same time. Of course she hadn't. It seemed so obvious now. She should have known. But she hadn't, not just because of her inadequacies, but because he had been so…ordinary.

Normal.

Casual.

Then, without any apparent change in his manner, Percy turned fast, kicking at Trina's hand before it could stray to the hilt of her sword. In fact, she hadn't even thought to move for it. The truth had paralyzed her, and she couldn't even defend herself.

Her stunned realization lasted only the merest fraction of a second, but it was enough to cost her everything. His spiteful, venomous kick caught her in the gut, and she crumpled off balance and winded. The savagery of the attack shredded her uncertainty, however, and woke her up to what was happening, or maybe it triggered some self-preservation instinct that was part her and part warrior angel. In either case, she shrugged her discomfort off and leapt to her feet, her mind playing catch up.

He was unarmed, or seemed to be.

The same thought appeared to strike him because he did not stay to fight. Instead, he kicked the sword away from her before she could reach it, sending it skittering across the floor, spinning on the wooden boards. Then he was bounding out of the room and slamming the heavy oak door behind him. At last Trina gave chase, but she still felt like she was moving in slow motion and it was already far too late. Her senses felt muted, mind and body just a fraction delayed as she pounded clumsily after him. She heard the solid thunk of the lock before she hit the door, and though she pounded on it with her fists, it didn't so much as shake.

Unable to catch him or stop whatever he was planning to do next, all her resolve left her in a wash of futility and despair, and in its place a single question rose to her lips, like the glow of her sword as it came to the surface of the lake.

"Why?" she gasped, tears breaking free and running down her face as she thought of the boy she had liked, all the unspeakable things he had done and the things he still intended to do. *"Why?"*

15

S he wasn't sure how long she stood at the locked door of the lighthouse keeper's cottage. It might only have been a few seconds, but it felt longer. She heard Percy walk away, whistling dryly through his teeth again, then heard his feet on the stairs up the tower itself, and then nothing. She could not answer the question she had thrown at him as he left, locking her inside,

Why?

but neither could she make sense of his guilt. Was he some kind of henchman, serving the Soulless One, or was he —somehow—the monster itself? He was just a kid like her. The creature who had blasted the chapel apart and killed all those people at the dance had been a thing of nightmares, a bird-headed figure out of the medieval hellscapes painted by Hieronymus Bosch.

It made no sense.

"*I am sorry,*" said the angel warrior.

The unexpected reminder of the spirit's presence within her stopped Trina's internal monologue in its tracks, though it did not bring the calm she might have expected.

"You knew," she said.

It wasn't a question.

The angel was silent.

"You knew," Trina repeated, "and you said nothing."

"*I could not. This is a human matter.*"

"How convenient for you."

"*I am sorry.*"

"Yeah," said Trina venomously. "You said."

"*I have given you the skills to fight back. I told you what you needed to know when you needed to know it. I told you when to run, when to hide, and when to fight.*"

"Maybe," said Trina, still hurt and angry. "But you didn't help me stop the massacre at the dance, and I had to get the sword myself. You didn't even heal me when I got hurt. That was the lady in the lake. So all you have actually done is convince me to fight when I should have run and given me just enough to make me a target. Worse, you've given me the urge to stop the enemy but not the power to do it. All I really have is a sense of complete and utter failure, of guilt."

Trina waited, but the angel was silent.

"Yeah," she said aloud. "That's what I thought."

She rattled the door handle one last time, but it stayed as solidly locked as before. Her eyes flashed around the room. The windows were small and high, but the one in the kitchen had been larger. It wouldn't get her into the tower, the external door to which he would surely have locked, but if she could get outside...

"*The ladder,*" said the angel softly.

Trina paused again, picturing the rickety structure up the side of the lighthouse. It had been ramshackle and rusty, and that was just the part she had seen. The top might be worse, or nonexistent. But she knew she had no choice.

"Right," she said wearily. "Of course."

She stooped and picked up the fallen sword, dragging its

tip along the floor as she went back into the kitchen.

The window over the counter was definitely large enough to climb through, but it was now so dark outside that she could make out nothing beyond the glass. She chose a cast iron pan, which was hanging over the stove, and heaved it roughly through the window. The glass exploded outward. She cleared some of the more lethal-looking shards from the frame with her sword, then climbed gingerly onto the counter.

It was a longer drop from the window than she had expected, but the grass below was lush and cushioned her fall. She moved around the outer walls of the cottage until she could see the barrel-shaped tower properly and looked up. It was some sixty or seventy feet high and tapered slightly. Near the top was a ledge, which ran all the way around, and above it was what she had been too close to the tower to see before: it resembled an oversized lantern with an iron frame. In fact, it was probably a glass-walled room only three or four yards across. There was a light on inside, but it was dim, a work light, not the beacon itself, and by its glow, she could make out the shadow and silhouette of movement.

He was up there. She wasn't sure what he was doing, but she could make a guess and knew she had to stop him. Trina had seen what the staff of power could do. If it was amplified somehow, borrowing energy from the lighthouse, amplifying it with the beacon's massive lenses, the destructive force of the thing might be immense, its range multiplied many times over.

Trina tried the outside door but, as expected, it was locked and bolted tight. Would he remember the ladder up the side? She had to hope not. If he was waiting for her at the top, she was dead, whether or not she was impervious to the weapon he wielded.

The thought gave her pause, not because she feared for her life, but she suddenly wondered if the necklace really made her invulnerable. It was Percy who had told her that, after all. If it protected her from him, why would he have given it to her in the first place?

"He did not."

Trina's mind reeled.

"What?"

"He told you he had sent the necklace to you, but that was a lie. He just wanted to get to know you once he knew you had it."

Trina closed her eyes and pressed the heel of her hand to her forehead, competing impossibilities racing though her head.

"So, who sent it?" she said at last. "If it wasn't Percy, then who?"

"I cannot tell you that," said the angel.

"More secrets? How am I supposed to fight if I only know half the story?"

"I cannot tell you," said the angel more gently, *"because I do not know. The necklace came into your possession, and I came with it."*

"Wait," said Trina as the full weight of this struck her, "so you didn't *choose* me?"

There was a loaded silence, and then the angel said simply, *"No."*

There was a stunned silence.

"So, I'm not special," said Trina, her heart breaking as all her old instincts returned and told her what she had always believed. "I'm nobody. And if someone else had the necklace, they'd be the one fighting to save everyone."

"It came to you."

"By accident!"

"You do not know that."

"I wasn't chosen. I never am. I'm just…me."

"That is sufficient."

Trina hung her head in despair and disbelief. She had never been sufficient before. Why should she think she was now? In response, the angel said nothing, and the silence between them dragged on. Somewhere out over the lake a bird called, eerie and distant, like a creature out of a fairy story. Trina sighed and shrugged.

"Okay," she said.

It wasn't acceptance of what the angel had said. It wasn't even a statement of resolution. It was acceptance that while any attempt to stop the monster in the lighthouse was almost certainly pointless, there was no one else there to make the attempt. Someone had to, and it seemed that someone was her.

"Okay," she said again.

She looked up the tower to the light and saw that the movement she had glimpsed within the beacon was different. So, for that matter, was the light itself. It was greenish, brighter than it had been, though it had nothing like the power she had seen from the staff before, and it looked to go straight up through the top of the lantern, dissipating into the night sky. A hatch had been opened on the roof. The shadows moved, and she could see that standing now on the very top of the lighthouse was the bird-headed creature. She would not think of him as Percy, and not only because she still did not understand how he could actually be the monster himself, she refused to give the creature a human face.

The Soulless One stood tall, legs spread wide, his staff of power upright in his hands as if he was fitting it into some mechanism within the beacon. Percy had said the lenses and mirrors would form part of his device, though the claim that this had been to break down the barrier around the town was clearly a lie. If his actions were the next stage of whatever had been raining devastation down on the forest by the lake, it might well be enough to wipe Treysville off the map entirely.

But he was still preparing the weapon, and that meant there might yet be a chance…

He paused in his work, and Trina felt his cold eyes find her in the thin glow of the gas lamp by the door. Her presence obviously alarmed him, and he stopped what he was doing, moving quickly to the very edge of the roof. With a sudden vengeful jab, he aimed the staff down at her. Its lightning crackled and exploded in a lethal streak of emerald fire. The ground a yard to Trina's right exploded, throwing grass and rubble every which way, but she stood her ground, sweeping the Destiny Sword up into her hands.

The Soulless One adjusted his aim, and this time she felt sure the lightning fire would hit her directly long before she could make it up the ladder to meet him in close combat, but Trina did not flinch. Instead, she focused on the gem in the hilt of her sword, unbidden by the angel, instinctively knowing what to do.

She opened it with her mind.

Then she stepped into the energy stream he had unleashed, catching it directly in the sword.

The dreadful shaft of electric power lancing toward her was sucked into the heart of the sword and held. Trina raised the blade, fighting to hold it steady, as the Soulless One increased the power coming at her, trying to wrench it from her grasp. She held on, sweat mingling with the lake water running down her face and arms, keeping the sword aloft even as the monster tried to redirect it. She held on, feeling the gem fill with power, gripping it as much with her mind as with her hands, and then she sent it streaming back, not green now but blue-white. It reversed course, streaking up the tower, and she felt the bird-thing's fury as it slammed into the staff and knocked him backward.

Yes, she thought. *I am Trina Warren. I am impervious.*

For a moment he lay crumpled on the top, but then he was moving again, abandoning the fight and returning to whatever task he had been about before he saw her. He adjusted something, then descended through the hatch into the beacon room itself, and though she could make out his silhouette moving around, she could not see what he was doing. She had the merest sliver of time before the fury of his staff, terribly magnified by the lighthouse, would be unleashed on the town.

Trina thrust the sword into her belt, grabbed hold of the metal upright of the makeshift ladder, feeling the rust flake under her palms, and began to climb. She moved steadily, hand over hand, her face as close to the mottled stone of the tower as she could get so that she wouldn't look down: five feet, ten, twenty, forty. There was a breeze up here and—still being in her wet clothes—it chilled her to the bone. When she reached the ledge below the light itself, she paused. There was the hatch at the top, but he would have locked it again as he climbed back inside. She considered the glass panels of the light casing, and her right hand went to the hilt of her sword.

Yes, she thought.

She drew it slowly, feeling her past life crowding in on her, certain beyond any measure that the next few seconds would define her existence.

"Percy is but my factor, good my lord..." she thought. *He may not have intended it this way*, she thought, *but he has made me what I am: his nemesis.*

The sword felt light as ever, a natural extension of her arm, something she had been meant to use. It still felt true even though she knew in her heart that it was a lie. She had not been chosen. The sword would feel like this to whoever had it. It was not a blade of destiny after all. It had merely come to her.

Well, she thought resignedly, *that was just how things went. You used what you had as well as you could. You made the best of it. What else was there?*

And so thinking, she reached back and drove the pommel of the sword into the window pane over her head.

In the split second before the glass shattered, Trina saw in, saw the shadowy movement of the Soulless One with his great beaked head and his staff of power, saw the contraption at the center of the lighthouse beacon, nestled in the ring of mirrors and lenses. They reflected themselves endlessly like a vortex, a spiraling passage to infinity at the heart of which sat a red plastic chair with chrome legs spinning in the moment of its eternal fall.

Then the glass was cascading down, splitting with a crash like a rifle shot. The cracks in the window radiated out across every panel, but somehow leapt to the lenses and mirrors and shutters of the beacon itself, crisscrossing like filigree then opening, swallowing, devouring everything. They coursed down the lighthouse tower itself, cleaving it in pieces till it fractured and fell. They ruptured the ground itself like an earthquake, ripping it up like a million jackhammers, splitting the Kitchener estate into fragments that collapsed in on themselves and evaporated. The lake drained in torrents and surges. The castle crumbled, and its battlements fell as if finally succumbing to the siege it had never faced. And still the cracks spread, ripping through forest and valley, cleaving the very air. The hills and caves, chapels and shops were riven with a spider web of fault lines, and then they too were crumbling into rubble and dust.

Rubble and dust, and then nothing.

Trina smashed the glass, and she broke the world.

16

The panel kicked out at one corner, and Trina pushed it till the thin metal folded back on itself and she was able to slip through, dropping down from the heating and air duct and landing hard on her ankle, so that it shrieked in protest. She huddled in a crouch, alarmed and disoriented. And then her eyes fell on the red chairs with the chrome legs. A ring of them, like an ancient stone circle, one of them pushed out of position and upended.

It wasn't moving now. Its unlikely spinning, tumbling fall, was over, and it lay on its side as if shot.

Shot.

The word sparked in her head, pulsing with red-hot energy and panic. Very slowly, she looked up.

The lighthouse was gone. She was in a familiar institutional building with cinderblock walls and a high, corrugated roof. The world was dimmer than it had been, somehow flatter and less vibrant. Trina also felt reduced, her senses muted, her former poise and balance gone. She stared at the parquet floor as she gathered herself. It was marked with painted lines, in the center of which was a golden lion reared up on its hind legs, roaring and pawing the air.

The Treys East High Lion. Their school mascot.

Trina stared at it, and something stirred in her memory. That was what they all were, the students: lions. That's what she was.

But she had seen the lion at the Kitchener estate and at the chapel. Even at the lighthouse.

She frowned, and her gaze strayed to the chair beside the lion.

It was the same as the others, red with chrome legs. It was where she had glimpsed it when all this stuff had started. Then it had been spinning, upended by the chaos she had fled from, glimpsed through the open doors as she and Jasmine had been walking to class. A whole circle of chairs, but only that one on its side. Trina stared at it, knowing there was some other horror she was not yet remembering.

She had been out there in the hallway with Jasmine. And now she was back, all her strange, impossible wanderings, all her adventures, had led her back to where it had all begun, though now she was on the inside of the doors.

How long had passed since then. An hour? Less? Much less.

She looked up. When she had first come in through the HVAC panel, she had thought the assembly hall was empty because it was so quiet, but now she saw huddles of kids in the corners, all squatting or sitting, their knees drawn up tight, their phones in their hands, but utterly silent. Dozens of them. They had locked themselves in here when the madness started. Gradually they all looked up to stare at her, eyes wide. One of them, a senior whose name she didn't know laid an unsteady finger on her lips and gave her a long, desperate look. They all had some form of that look, though some had buried it deeper and looked merely blank. Most looked wild. Terrified.

The silence was broken by a popping bang from somewhere down the hall, followed quickly by another.

A ripple passed through the huddled students. Trina actually saw it like a shock wave moving through them as they winced and crouched lower, burying their faces in their hands. Then came the gasps, the badly stifled sobs, interrupted and heightened by another bang, closer this time.

A shot, said her brain again. *Not a mystical staff of power. A gun.*

She moved to the nearest group, a silent, loping run that kept her low to the ground. She didn't realize who was there until she reached them.

"Where have you been?" mouthed Jasmine. She looked distraught, her face tear streaked, but she was also just confused. Trina's clothes and hair were dripping wet. "I texted you! I thought you were dead."

The girl who had put her finger to her lips did it again emphatically, but the gesture was not so much scolding as pleading. She too was weeping soundlessly. Trina plucked her phone from her pocket, but it was full of water and utterly dead. She looked at Jasmine's phone, as if she had never seen one before. It showed updating news bulletins from all the local networks and a flashing message from the school's emergency alert system:

Active shooter: Run. Hide. Fight.

Trina stared at it. They were the first things the angel had told her.

Where have you been?

"I went to the chapel," Trina replied at last in a whisper, stringing it altogether like beads on a necklace. "I mean the Quiet Room. There were models of knights and a dragon." She thought of the discarded effigies from someone's school project and how she had somehow made them real in her head, and she blinked and shook her head. "But then he came," she said. "I ran to the caves…"

Jasmine gave her a blank look.

"Not the caves," Trina corrected, trying to focus, remembering how the stone had felt like tile and smelled of body odor and bleach. "The changing rooms by the gym. But he came there too. I hid, and then… Then I went…" She fought to make sense of it all in her head, but the pieces wouldn't fit. "I wanted to go home, but I couldn't get out, so I went to the Kitchener estate…"

Another bewildered look.

"The Kitchener…" Trina began, then paused. "The *kitchens*. I went to the kitchens to find a weapon, but I couldn't get through and…"

"You were in the cafeteria?" hissed Jasmine, her eyes horrified.

Trina stared at her.

Had she been? She wasn't sure. She thought of the ballroom with its overtones of familiar, institutional food.

"We heard the shots," said Jasmine. "The screaming."

"Yes," said Trina, devastated by the realization but still vague, as if newly woken from a dream. "I *was* there."

"Did you see who…was hurt?" Jasmine began.

Candace, thought Trina, but she couldn't say that. Not now.

"A lot of people," she said. "Too many."

"How did you get out?"

Trina scowled and stared at nothing. Even so, her eyes fell on one of the ravaged brochures laid out by the kids trying to raise money for the DC trip. Their tables—one of which Jasmine had said was like a pawnshop because of the jewelry they had for sale—had been just outside this room. Her gaze lingered on the glossy images from the Smithsonian, the sea dragon and the doubled-tusked narwhal...

"Trina?" Jasmine prompted.

"I ran," she said, piecing the truth of it together in her head as she spoke, as if she were stringing beads for a necklace. She thought of the black waters of the lake, the strange, chemical smell. "I ran down to the pool," she said, only now reaching for the sword she had stowed in her belt. She drew it, realizing as she did so that it was shorter than she had expected. Its handle was soft and black, streaked with yellow.

Plastic, she thought dimly.

Its metal blade was thick and tapered, only a foot or so long and coming to a sharp point. Its lower edge was jagged with keen, even serrations.

A sheetrock saw. That was what it was called. You used it to carve wall board. There was construction work happening around the pool. She remembered now.

"I found this," she said dreamily. "I guess one of the workers had left it and it got kicked into the water when he..." She thought of the bodies in the lake. The hole in her shoulder seemed to reopen at the memory so that she winced and clapped her free hand to the wound.

"You're hit!" whispered Jasmine, covering first her mouth and then her eyes, as if trying to shut out the horror.

"I was in the water," Trina mused. "I dreamed of my mother. I must have been unconscious..." Her eyes strayed to the ring of chairs, the only place no one was sitting. Something was lying inside the ring, half hidden by the chairs. It had looked merely like an untidy heap of fabric, but she knew what it was now. A boy. Lying on his back, a jacket draped respectfully over his face.

"Who is that?" she said.

Jasmine shook her head emphatically.

"Don't look," she said.

But Trina stood up, moved lightly over to the corpse, and stooped to it. She raised the jacket, taking in the horror of what she saw.

It was the boy with the gold-rimmed glasses and blank eyes, the one she had seen at the dance before the massacre, the one who had given her the egg and then had said something awful.

"Trina. This is on you."

She understood now. He had been with her in the hallway when it had started. She had been arguing with him. He had wanted to get in here for some club or meeting, but she had been in his way. When he had called her on it, she had called him rude.

And then he had been hit. She had forgotten that part, but she saw it now. She had heard the shot without realizing what it was. Someone had screamed and, as the running started, as she had been separated from Jasmine in the stampede, he had gone down, eyes open but empty, one hand held up above the crowd, fingers splayed and rigid. He had been the first, and if he hadn't been standing arguing with her, he would have made it inside alive. He had stumbled in here before the doors were locked, spilling the table with its brochures, and he had upended the little plastic chair that had been sitting in the center of the room like part of an ancient stone circle. Instead, he was lying in the corner with a jacket draped over his face, those gold-rimmed glasses very slightly out of place so that his face looked twisted.

The truth of the realization stung like a fire brand, like a horn through the shoulder.

Like a bullet.

She thought it again: If she hadn't kept him standing there when the shooting started, he might still be alive. And maybe she wouldn't.

That was why she had been feeling guilty. Not because it

was her fault. Not because he had died, but because she hadn't. It could have been either of them, their lives dependent on a coin toss or which corsage they chose...

That hand stretching for the ceiling, fingers splayed...

"I'm sorry," Trina said softly. "You were right. It was my fault. I didn't mean to..."

"Shh!" hissed the senior girl. Trina locked eyes with her, and through her terror, the girl was just able to mouth, "He's coming."

Trina gathered herself instinctively into a coiled crouch, eyes on the double doors into the hall. They had reinforced glass panels at chest height. The knife-saw in her hand sang to her, and her left hand went to the necklace at her throat.

It wasn't there.

Trina stared, horror struck.

She must have lost it in the lake

Pool

Or crawling through the culvert

HVAC ducts.

Maybe she had lost it as she scaled the lighthouse itself.

Except that there had been no lighthouse. She had made it all up. The necklace was gone, and she was ordinary again. No wonder the world felt so flat, so muted. No wonder she felt clumsy and useless again. The necklace was gone and that meant that she was dead or would be very soon. It might look like she was talking and breathing, but to all intents and purposes, she was dead. She just hadn't accepted it yet.

Pronounced dead at the scene, she thought vaguely, seeing the headlines, though not the number that proceeded them.

He's coming...

"Percy," she whispered to no one.

"Who?" said Jasmine.

"The..." Trina sought for the word. "The shooter," she said. "Percy."

Even through her grief and horror, Jasmine's face twisted with confusion.

"His name's Brad," she said. "He's a senior. I don't know him, but on Twitter they're saying…"

"*Shh!*" hissed the senior girl.

Trina stared at Jasmine.

Brad?

The name meant nothing to her. So, her conversations with Percy, her sense of his helping her, all of it, she had made up. Trina stared at Jasmine, and the longer she crouched there, the more she felt that what she had been told had left her somehow paralyzed. Dimly she became aware of pressure in her hip pocket and reached in, pulling out a brass cylinder some three inches long, what she had imagined to be a talisman. It was a spent shell casing. Of course it was. She could even smell the gunpowder off it. The classrooms and hallways were probably strewn with them. Shells and bodies.

Trina put the knife down.

Another shot from outside, closer still. It was loud, but it was a flat sound, no more intense than a car door slamming. It wasn't like the movies at all. They added all that reverb that made it sound so much cooler, so much more significant. This sounded stupid. Trivial.

Casual.

She considered the word, and suddenly she knew what she was going to hear next. First, the footsteps, slow and easy, the footfalls of someone who felt comfortable and in control.

They stopped outside the double doors, and something loomed into view through the glass, something familiar and impossible.

A bird head.

It was the size of a man, but there was no question what it was. Or who. Trina saw the long, arcing beak.

The Soulless One. Percy.

The students shrank away. Some typed their final texts and slipped their phones in their pockets.

Trina listened. At first she couldn't make it out, but then she caught it, the faint, breathy hum of someone whistling between his teeth.

He tried the latch quietly at first, then again, rougher. He kicked at the doors, and they shook in their frames.

Trina heard him take a step and realized what was going to happen. She waved wildly at two girls who were directly opposite the doors, motioning them toward the corner. They gaped at her, incapable of moving.

She expected the first shot to punch the lock from the center of the doors, but that was another movie convention. The first shot went high into the right corner, blowing out a ragged hole and sending splinters and shrapnel cannoning across the hall. Trina didn't realize what was happening till the second shot came, carefully positioned a few feet lower.

Directly on the hinge.

His shoulder charge broke the right-hand door open, not at the central latch, but against the jamb itself. And then he was through, the Soulless One, his great beak swinging from side to side as he scanned for targets with his staff of power, though that was not the sleek and exotic brand spewing lightning and fiery purple spheres. It was a rifle, black and purposeful. Deadly, but ordinary.

And Trina, equally ordinary Trina, ungifted by angel warrior spirits, was frozen in fear. She was, she knew, impervious no more, and the only questions were who he would kill first and who he would kill last, and neither seemed to matter very much.

But he didn't shoot right away. He whistled, drinking in

their fear, and she saw now that the bird head was only a carnival mask, one she remembered from her history project on the Black Death. She gaped, and he, as if reading her thoughts, spoke. Immediately she knew that though his real name might be Brad, he was the person she had been imagining as Percy. Why she had given a boy she didn't know a name out of legends and history she couldn't say.

Not that it mattered now.

"I am the Plague Doctor," Percy said to the room, and she realized she had heard him make this speech before, in the hallway, perhaps, or the cafeteria. A grand speech it was, but also a kind of private joke. "But I come not to cure the diseases of humanity. I bring them. I am the plague. I am the Black Death. *Anima Absentia*: the Soulless One."

Trina blinked. His voice was muffled by the mask, but over the shouting and the crying, he was like the gun, which should have been powerful and dramatic but wasn't. He was posturing, and for all the awfulness of what he was doing, he was absurd.

But then so was she. She wasn't Captain Marvel, Xena, or Wonder Woman. All her fantasies of heroism and battle were suddenly laid bare, revealed as the smoke and mirrors of evasion and self-deception. There had been no battle in the pawnshop, no life and death struggle in the chapel. There had only ever been this.

He wasn't even injured. There was no seeping wetness above his belt buckle. She must have made that up too. She had made a lot of things up, but most of them had been analogies to what was really happening, ways of making reality bearable. She saw that now. She had dipped into her fantasy life because it made more sense than the place she actually lived. But the belly wound: that had been a lie, a self-deception that might offer hope when his mask came off.

He was whole and unscathed. The wounds, the awful,

unspeakable wounds that Trina had seen and rationalized so she wouldn't go mad with horror at the nature of reality, those all belonged to other people, and they were his doing. The casual arrogance of it made her weep and rage all at once. His speechifying might be stupid, but it confirmed what she had instinctively known: none of them could expect any kind of mercy from him. She did not know why in her imaginary version of events she had seen him as a helper, someone facilitating her heroism.

All this unfolded in her mind in seconds, though it seemed to take much longer. Around her there was crying while Percy—*Brad*—talked, covering them with his rifle from the doorway, savoring their terror and his moment of power over them, but Trina felt oddly calm. Perhaps it was all she had been through that had left her inured to panic. Perhaps it was that it was all so pitifully mundane. After all, things like this happened every day in America. Today just happened to be Treysville's turn. If the body count didn't break records, they'd only be news for a day or two. She felt Jasmine cling to her, hiding her face in Trina's wet clothes, and in doing so, she dislodged something that spilled out of her soaking pocket and rolled in front of her.

It was the plastic egg, sky blue, like something you might buy in a drug store at Easter to fill with candy.

It spun and wobbled, but Trina put her hand on it, baffled, and remembered slowly. Her eyes flashed to the corpse of the spectacled boy who lay by the chair he had overturned. In her fugue-state or whatever the fantasy world she had imagined had been, he had given her the egg. But he couldn't have. Not really. She had invented that too, but it had felt significant when he gave it to her, and when she had moved to open it, he had told her not to.

"Not till the very end."

Well, she thought, *that is now.*

She stared at the pale blue egg, and suddenly she smelled cotton candy and oil. She heard laughter and the hurdy-gurdy whine of carousel music. Perplexed, she turned the egg over in her hand and saw where it was marked in crude, black sharpie:

Treysville annual fair.

She remembered her father's whoop of delight when he had won it for her, celebrating so much that the wry stall owner couldn't help but grin as he handed over the prize.

Not till the very end.

She put her thumbnails into the crack and opened it.

Inside was a cheap silver necklace with a tiny sword pendant.

Of course.

Trina stared, her eyes filling with tears, remembering and understanding. There was no angel but her. There never had been.

So she decided. She lifted the chain out of the egg and passed it around her neck, sensing that hers was the only movement in the room. Her hand groped for the sheetrock saw, found it, picked it up silently. Percy was ranting about why he was doing what he was doing, and Trina found that, unexpectedly, she didn't care. What possible blend of disaffected whining and entitlement could excuse what he had done or was about to do? His reasons didn't matter. He didn't matter.

Percy is but my factor, she thought, the Shakespeare lines coming unbidden to her mind like tears, the words adjusting as she made them hers:

And in the closing of some glorious day
I will be bold to say I am your daughter;
When I will wear a garment all of blood
And stain my favors in a bloody mask,
Which, wash'd away, shall scour my shame with it.

And then she was up and running, and the surprise of her attack almost made him miss, but he could not stop the upward sweep of her sword into his belly so that he went down hard and would not come up again.

Then there was only Jasmine, weeping over her dying friend. Trina lay still, smiling sadly through her pain, trying to say that it was okay. That she was fine. Better than that.

She was impervious.

And then she was gone.

THE END

AFTERWORD

When I was ten or eleven, I wrote a story for class about a tiger loose in my school. It was a kid's adventure, full of daring and excitement, or so I remember it. I've always loved those kinds of stories, but as I've gotten older, I've come to see that the real danger to people is generally not wild animals so much as it is other people, people equipped with instruments of death manufactured and sold with fewer safeguards and regulations than, say, a car.

I began thinking about this more human story several years ago and created a couple of different outlines for the novel, but my work on other projects kept it on the back burner. On Tuesday, April 30th, 2019, I was on the campus of the university where I teach—UNC Charlotte—for an end of year celebration honoring graduating seniors, when a gunman opened fire in a neighboring building. I took cover with a group of students in a theatre dressing room and we locked ourselves in. We sat in silence for something over an hour, watching on muted phones—we couldn't make any noise for fear of attracting the shooter—for local news reports that might help us make sense of what was happening outside. By the time we got the all-clear from the police, two students had been killed and several others seriously wounded. The scars borne by the survivors are less easy to quantify.

So yes, I wrote this book in direct response to the shooting, throwing out all but the premise of my earlier outlines and drafting it in two weeks before my sense of the experience faded. Because that's what they do, these expressly American mass shootings: they fade, maybe not from the lives of the people impacted by them, but in the minds of the general public. We send our thoughts and prayers, say how terrible it is, and ignore the plain and obvious fact that this is a distinctly American problem that is indisputably connected to the wide availability of firearms. Some people will doubtless object that a novel is not a place for political polemic, but that seems to me a misunderstanding of the nature and power of art, which is always and has always been political, if only indirectly. Art is and always has been political. Every book (or movie, or TV show) that glorifies gun violence and feeds the pathological craving to own instruments designed expressly to kill is making a political statement, however tacitly. This is mine.

Every major study suggests the same hard truths: that the presence of guns directly contributes to homicide rates and in particular to mass homicides. Statistics also show that people who own guns for their own protection are more likely to die by those same weapons. But lastly, and more positively, it is also self-evident that countries which have chosen to take the restriction of gun ownership seriously have successfully reduced the possibility of these kinds of atrocities happening again.

It just takes some political will, and the shelving of some outdated laws.

And here's the thing; I have been saying the same things

about US gun laws for literally decades, and the worst thing about the experience I had on campus is that it felt so completely ordinary, so everyday. The one thing that changed for me this time was the new realization that these incidents don't just happen to other people. There is a good chance they will happen to you or the people you love. Maybe not in a school: maybe in a mall, or a movie theatre, or a nightclub, or a sports stadium, or a church. Nowhere is safe. Think about that, because it is absolutely true. It can happen literally anywhere because evil really is arbitrary and indiscriminate. We can't fix that, but we can make it considerably harder for people to get hold of their preferred choice of killing device. Because while heroism, goodness, and self sacrifice are real and powerful things, you can't expect them to always win out like they do in the movies, and you really need to get past the idea that mass shootings only happen to other people. Please hear this. We need to address our pathological fascination with guns because bullets kill: simple as that, and no one

NO ONE

is impervious.

ACKNOWLEDGMENTS

This was, obviously, a very personal book to write—one that I had to write as a way of working through the experience—so I'm in debt to those early readers who helped me gauge whether it might be worth sharing with the world. Special thanks to Finie Osako, Stacey Glick, David Coe, Kerra Bolton, Ola Jacunski, Faith Hunter, Carrie Ryan, Misty Massey, and Sebastian Hartley, as well as to two of the students who sheltered with me that day, Thurston Williams and Jack Murphy, who read an early draft of the book. The book is dedicated to the memories of those who died.

ABOUT THE AUTHOR

A.J. Hartley (also writing as Andrew Hart) is the international bestselling author of over twenty novels, including the award-winning *Steeplejack* series; *Lies That Bind Us* (thriller), *Cold Bath Street* (a ghost story), *Cathedrals of Glass* (scifi), and the *Sekret Machines* series, (co-written with Blink 182 front man, Tom DeLonge).

He was born in northern England, but has lived in many places including Japan, and is currently the Robinson Professor of Shakespeare studies at the University of North Carolina, Charlotte, where he specializes in the performance history, theory and criticism of Renaissance English drama, and works as a director and dramaturg.

ALSO BY A.J. HARTLEY

(As Andrew Hart)

Lies That Bind Us

The Woman In Our House

Preston Oldcorn Series

Cold Bath Street

Written Stone Lane

Will Hawthorne Series

Act of Will

Will Power

Sekret Machines (with Tom DeLonge)

Chasing Shadows

A Fire Within

Cathedrals of Glass (with Tom DeLonge)

A Planet of Blood and Ice

SteepleJack

Steeplejack

Firebrand

Guardian

Hamlet, Prince of Denmark: A Novel (with David Hewson)

Macbeth: A Novel (with David Hewson)

Mask of Atreus

What Time Devours

On The Fifth Day

Tears of the Jaguar

FALSTAFF BOOKS

**Want to know what's new
And coming soon from
Falstaff Books?**

Try This Free Ebook Sampler

https://www.instafreebie.com/free/bsZnl

**Follow the link.
Download the file.**
Transfer to your e-reader, phone, tablet, watch, computer,
whatever.
Enjoy.

PATRONS

Thank You to All our Falstaff Books Patrons, who get extra digital content each month! To be featured here and see what other great rewards we offer, go to www.patreon.com/falstaffbooks.

PATRONS

Dino Hicks
John Hooks
John Kilgallon
Larissa Lichty
Travis & Casey Schilling
Staci-Leigh Santore
Sheryl R. Hayes
Scott Norris
Samuel Montgomery-Blinn
Junkle

Made in the USA
Columbia, SC
29 April 2020